BLVD. *of* BLOOD

BLVD. *of* BLOOD

a suspense-thriller by

Hal Johnson

PUBLISHING

Blvd. of Blood

Spontaneous Combustion Publishing
Red Bank, NJ • Milford, CT • Brooklyn, NY
E.O.Y. 2025

for S. H. S.

Cottinend, N.Y., 201—
the itinerary

plan your route

Evil thoughts can never be cherished, day after day, without leading the more daring or brutal into some form of crime.
•H. Irving Hancock, *The High School Captain of the Team* (1910).

I. THE PAWNS ASSEMBLE.

Colin Lang • Bernie Feldstein • Alan Jancewicz • Colin Lang • Bernie Feldstein • John Oberman • Colin Lang • more Colin Lang • Colin Lang yet again • John Oberman • Colin Lang • Delia Jancewicz • Bernie Feldstein • Colin Lang • Bernie Feldstein • Colin Lang • Carol Wernick • Bernie Feldstein • Colin Lang • John Oberman • Colin Lang

1 Twenty years passed after his last arrest before Colin Lang began to think about killing someone. ¶ In adolescence, Colin had been a little wild—just the usual high-spirits of any high school boy, really: underage beer parties and vandalism. An older kid in shop class taught Colin how to hot-wire a car, and he went joyriding in his neighbors' vehicles once or twice. Mostly, though, it was beer and mailboxes, but even the mild vandalism of mailbox baseball could get you sentenced to community service, if you, or your friends, were stupid when you did it. Underage beer made his friends stupid, and Colin got caught a couple of times. The cops brought out the handcuffs; the judge hammered his gavel. It was all designed to strike fear into Colin's young soul, but he knew that he'd get off with a few weekends picking up trash in a park. Nothing to worry about.

But there was that final time. Colin had been driving around at night, drunk, with six friends in his neighbors' stolen minivan. None of them had had a car large enough to fit the seven of them, so stealing a minivan had seemed like a good idea, and they couldn't have even been speeding much, but—

The siren in the rearview. With seven total perpetrators, the cops ran out of handcuffs. Four boys got stuffed in the backseat of the cop car, but Colin was just standing idly by while the cops searched the minivan unsuccessfully for drugs. And while Colin stood there he noticed that the keys, the cops had left their keys.

In the ignition.

What happened next was (Colin's lawyer later explained) a momentary lapse in judgment. It was a lapse in judgment that took Colin and his friends, all seven of them jammed on laps into the cop car, on a wild race across several counties and two states before Colin instinctively swerved to dodge a jogger, careening through a guard rail and off a low embankment into a marsh. This was suddenly something more serious than a swiped stop sign or a broken window. Colin was seventeen, and being tried as an adult was a real danger. Apparently driving a stolen cop car across state lines and wrecking it in Pennsylvania was frowned upon by the penal code. The road map the district attorney's assistant laid out was a tangle of forbidding words and phrases: from "federal offense" through "hard time" to a ruined life, its shambles swept up into a halfway house.

Colin's parents were wealthy enough to hire a good lawyer, though, and Colin admittedly dressed up very well. In the end, the case never made it to court, and Colin never went to prison. For the first time, though, prison had seemed very real. "Scared straight," Colin learned to say to the mandatory counselor, and he said it so many times it proved true. The youthful offense disappeared, like magic, from his record, and by that time Colin was already at a good college, studying for a good job, or at least a respectable one. By his mid twenties he was sitting at the actuarial consulting firm of Radcliffe Worth Partners and studying for his associate's exams. The rest of his life was easy to see, and it was much less terrifying than the one laid out by the D.A.'s office had been. It was also dull. It was smotheringly dull.

At thirty-five, Colin was an actuarial fellow, and he had a nice house, a nice dog (which soon died), a string of unsuccessful relationships, and a fat bank account. He could not complain, because any time he tried to complain someone said, "You have it all; you just need to find a nice girl." But nice girls did not stop him from being dead inside. He drove to work and he shook hands and he had a coffee mug with a cartoon pig on it and he was dead inside.

He tried skydiving, but he was dead inside. He tried Vegas, but he was dead inside. He saved up and tried booking, through a German company, a southeast Asian sex-junket, but he was dead inside.

One German tourist on the bus hinted broadly about a place in Russia where the very rich could hunt and kill prostitutes, but Colin knew he would never be able to save up enough for such a hunt. He thought back to the time he had stolen that cop car. He remembered the feeling of that long night into morning, a feeling he had not known since. He remembered his only regret: the jogger he had missed.

On his way to work, Colin began imagining that he might swerve his car into the bicycle lane, or a crowded sidewalk. What would happen? What could they do? He imagined people rolling up his car's hood to smash against his cob-webbed windshield and rebound away, their helpless limbs flailing. How many could he sweep through?

He would get caught of course; he would do hard time if he tried any of that. His only sensible recourse, after running over the pedestrians, would be to cut hard into oncoming traffic, take out another car head on, a last gesture of defiance. Unsatisfactory, that ending; but he thought about it, turning it over in his mind like a jeweler with an unworked stone, looking for facets to polish.

Or perhaps he could do something from a distance: find a railroad bridge and crowbar up the tracks right in the middle, so the train would pitch over the side. There was a fine bridge not far from his house in Cottinend; but it seemed to have only cargo trains. A waste of a good crowbarring.

There was a book he'd had to read in high school English class that he half remembered; he remembered an ax. He imagined picking a random house and smashing through the patio door with an ax while the family was watching TV. They'd turn their heads to see him emerging from a glittering cocoon of flying glass, and then the ax would be upon them. At the gym he imagined his hands were hoisting not dumbbells but an ax, and the ax fell again and again.

These were just thoughts, of course. Idle fantasies of the kind he used to have, as a kid, about naked actresses, or Bond villains. Castles, he would have said to a counselor if a counselor had still been mandatory, in the air.

Soon he had no one to say it to. Those few friends he'd had drifted away. His coworkers he nodded to and smiled at, but nothing more. "Competent and professional," they would have said about him.

He drove to work and he was dead inside. He called his mother on her birthday and he was dead inside. His dog died suddenly and he was still dead inside.

It was not until he met Bernie Feldstein that he bought the rifle.

2 In high school, the doctor told Bernie Feldstein that he had won the shit lottery, which was not a nice way to put it. People did not put things nicely to Bernie Feldstein. He was, perhaps, stupid, or perhaps he was simply not good at paying attention in school, but soon enough there was no difference between these two options. If you cannot pay attention in school they assume you are stupid, and put you in classes with stupid people until you're stupid by default. Bernie sat in the class for dumb kids and bad kids, unaware, as most of them were unaware, that some of the kids were just dumb and some of the kids were just bad, and the only way anyone knew how to treat any of them was to yell at them to sit still and be quiet.

Everything was terrible, of course; but Bernie didn't really understand it was terrible until the day Fernando Garcia arrived in town.

Bernie was in ninth grade at the time, when into the dumb kids' class, which was also the bad kids' class, came a new student. He was a recent immigrant from Mexico or (Bernie thought) somewhere like that, and he spoke very little English. He knew the words that were in movie titles, but that was it. *Striking Distance. Three on a Match. Bikini Bank Heist.* Nothing else. Welcome to the dumb kids, Fernando! Bernie didn't give it a second thought.

After a few months, though, Fernando's English improved, and he was taken out of Bernie's class. He was put in a regular class. Like the regular kids.

Bernie was furious! His lot in life was to suffer in the bad kids' class, the dumb kids' class, and if Fernando had also been assigned this lot—who was Fernando

4

to escape? Bernie decided that he would have revenge, and one day after school he jumped Fernando.

It was then that Bernie learned something about himself. He learned that he was not actually a "hard man." The ballpoint tattoos and murder music did not make him a hard man. He learned that the element of surprise was not sufficient to keep Fernando from getting the upper hand and beating him, decisively, up. Bernie was sent to one doctor for his mashed nose, and another to see why he had started a fight.

"You won the shit lottery," the second doctor told Bernie (somewhat unprofessionally) after a battery of tests. "If you'd've been a little bit dumber, you'd be in special ed., and no one would blame you. You'd be a good guy. And if you'd've been a little bit smarter, you'd be in the regular classes, and you'd be a good guy there too. But you're not quite dumb enough, and you're not quite smart enough, so you're always going to be the bad guy. Whatever trouble you're in is all your fault."

Everyone yelled at Bernie for the assault, but he forgot about that quickly. He would have gotten yelled at anyway. What he did not forget was the doctor's analysis. This analysis struck Bernie as grossly unfair, but, as it came from a doctor, he never thought to question it. The fact that he had missed out on special ed. haunted him. He wasn't sure what the special ed. room was like, but he came to believe that it was some kind of paradise. *A paradise he was barred from.* Were there arcade games in there? Was there a strip club? Oh, you might know the answer is *no*, but you are probably smarter than Bernie Feldstein. You probably know more about how the world works. You may know that the special ed. room is full of all sorts of kids with different needs, each one of whom won a private shit lottery. "In fact, everyone's won the shit lottery," you might want to tell him. "It's not just you." But nobody told him.

So Bernie stood outside the special ed. room, fuming. Eventually a hall monitor would drag him away, back to the dumb kids' class, the bad kids' class,

5

yelling at him all the way. And Bernie did what you might expect in this situation. He decided one day to jump one of the special ed. kids.

It was Alan Jancewicz; and that day Bernie was reminded of what he had forgotten. Bernie was not a hard man. Alan Jancewicz kicked his ass.

3 That was the only fight Alan Jancewicz had ever been in. He didn't get into trouble for it. Nothing changed because of it. He went to class, day after day. He graduated from high school, more or less. He grew up, but he was never going to be able to get a job, or live on his own. He lived with his parents. His sister left for college, so they got him a cat. He spent his days on his two passions, which were cars and porcelain frogs. He also watched game shows.

Alan had a problem with his brain, which had grown, in his adolescence, in a strange shape and to an uncomfortable size. Doctors had had to cut holes in his skull to accommodate the way his brain was growing. Metal plates covered the holes, and the scalp, re-sewn on, covered the plates; but of course the metal plates could not lie flush with the skull; his head, consequently, had a lumpy quality. The kids said he looked like an alien, which was cruel, but Alan didn't mind. Looking like an alien wasn't so bad. If he didn't collect little frog figurines, he might have collected little alien figurines.

Every morning his mother took him for a drive, so he could look at cars. Their route was precisely the same every morning. Up past the park, around through the Shopping District, and then down Blande Boulevard and home. They'd been doing it for years. And for the last six months, every morning as they drove down Blande Boulevard, they would pass, going the opposite direction, a man driving a car, a man Alan had seen now and again over the years, although they had only interacted once—not spoken, really, but interacted. That man was Bernie Feldstein, and his eyes, visibly from across a median, would track Alan's car; and they were smoking with hate.

4 Alcohol just made Colin feel dead inside, or deader inside, but it was an experiment he returned to every once in a while. He didn't like talking to people as he drank, though, so he varied the location. Here he was, sitting in a dark corner of the Munster Pub with shots lined up in front of him. It was after work so he was till dressed in his work clothes; he was dressed better than anyone else in the establishment. "Even the hookers," he thought, unkindly.

He was neither enjoying nor not enjoying the beginning of a drunken night, when a younger man sidled over. He was wearing a denim jacket with the sleeves ripped off, and a ratty goatee. He was carrying a chair. He looked eager to explain something.

It was a cold and desolate October, almost Halloween.

5 Bernie was a regular at the Munster. He'd told his stories too many times to every other denizen of the bar, so whenever a fresh ear wandered by, Bernie zeroed in. When he spotted the stranger, Bernie was already drunk—as he was, of course, every night. He didn't have to be at work until ten thirty A.M. now—his latest employer, a pizza parlor, opened at eleven, and someone else fired up the ovens—so there was no impetus to get home with only a light buzz. The sullen, gaunt stranger hardly looked like a promising audience: He was too well-dressed, too unfriendly, and probably a decade or two older than Bernie; his hair was parted precisely. But "any port in a storm," as Bernie's father used to say.

"Bernie," he said by way of introduction as he slid his seat over near stranger's table. "I won the shit lottery."

"Join the club," the man said. He said it absently, but as he said it he looked up, and his eye caught Bernie's. Was there something in Bernie's eyes, the shame and the rage? The impotent pain of someone who knows that if he started the fights he wanted to start he would lose instantly? What did the stranger see in him?

Must have been something. "Tell me about it," the man said. And the incoherent drunken rant that Bernie spewed out may have made little sense, but the stranger was nodding like a man who understood. The crappy job, the no girls, the long life of humiliation.

"Perhaps," the man ventured, "you're angry enough, you sometimes think about killing someone?"

Had Bernie mentioned that? He didn't remember mentioning it, but it was true. Bernie admitted he thought about shooting someone, shooting from one car and into another car, every day of his life. Every day on Blande Boulevard.

Blande Boulevard? The man stopped a moment. He might have been trying to orient himself. Probably he was not a lifer in Cottinend, as Bernie was. The long, dead stretch of Blande Boulevard, a gentle S-shaped curve with nothing but trees on either side.

"From car to car?" the man asked.

Yes.

"Do you have a gun yourself?"

Bernie did not.

"A car?"

Ah, that Bernie did. It was registered in Pennsylvania because that's where he'd bought it, and he'd never bothered to—

"Pennsylvania plates?" the man asked, cutting him off.

Indeed.

"Do you live alone?"

Once again, yes.

The man leaned in conspiratorially. He whispered close to Bernie's face a few short sentences. Then he added, "Bernie, my boy, you have been chosen for something important. Don't tell anyone about this conversation. Don't tell anyone about me. Write your name and address on this napkin. I'll come see you in..." (he glanced at his phone) "...six months." He named a day in April. April 10. "Make sure you're in, and alone. I'll come to you. Can you remember that date?"

"I'm not retarded," Bernie said.

"You've been chosen for big things," the man repeated. "Glorious destiny. You must keep this absolutely top secret. If you see me around town, you must not acknowledge me. My name is Theodore Anderson." He paid his bill with cash and left, perhaps a little faster than your average patron.

Bernie sat there nursing his beer slowly enough that he began to sober up. He wasn't sure whether Theodore Anderson worked for the military or the mafia, but he held both in equal reverence and didn't much care. By the time a weary waitress shook his shoulder and murmured: "Closing time," Bernie was stone cold sober.

6 John Oberman was some five years older than Bernie or Alan; he'd gone to the same high school, but had never heard about their fight. He'd never met either of them until that night in October.

Not that there were so many fights in Cottinend High. It probably was not a rough place, really, although to Oberman it seemed rough. It was a rough time in his life. His mother was a high-functioning alcoholic, and his father was just generally low-functioning. John Oberman wasn't very interested in most of his school subjects. His attempts to grow a mustache were unsuccessful and, he was told, pathetic. His best friend moved to Colorado. This one guy Bowen Mazzoli kept shoving him down. It was like an afterschool special except everyone was uglier.

Oberman was not a tattletale, and when Bowen pushed him down he just stood up again. Bowen sat two rows behind Oberman in Spanish class, and he used to shoot rubber bands at him. Probably he shot rubber bands at everyone.

But one day Bowen lobbed a hunk of gum over Trina Henderson's head and it landed in Oberman's hair. Even then, Oberman didn't narc. He just went to Señora Pierdowski and asked if he could go to the nurse so she could cut the gum out.

Señora Pierdowski somehow decided immediately that Oberman had put the gum into his own hair in a bid to get out of class. She sent him not to the nurse but to the vice principal, who acted as though Pierdowski had been an eyewitness to Oberman gumming himself. In addition to the usual punishments for "defrauding a teacher" and "goldbricking"—in addition to the detention and the call home to a tipsy mother—Mr. Carrithers told Oberman that he would have to see the school psychologist, because putting gum in your own hair was not only "weird" but also "a little fruity." Oberman lost one free period a week so he could listen to the psychologist, who was actually just the one school nurse with an extra summer of training, singsong platitudes to him. And all that day, through two periods and lunch and two more periods, Oberman had had to sit, at Carrithers's orders, red-faced with gum in his hair.

A sane man may have given up all belief in a benevolent authority. But Oberman decided that he would, as the poster on the nurse-psychiatrist's office wall said, BE THE CHANGE THAT YOU WANT TO SEE IN THE WORLD. He was not temperamentally suited for being an educator; and he would probably never be a politician; but there are many ways to serve for a single-minded young man. Oberman buckled down at school and came out the other end as a police recruit. He joined the force in the Village of Cottinend, one of forty officers, and by far the youngest.

Bowen Mazzoli still lived in Cottinend. He was a dentist. Sarah Pierdowski lived in Cottinend, too, and Carrithers right over the border in Hobsons Falls. Oberman always fantasized about pulling one of them over for a routine traffic violation. He'd see if they remembered him as he remembered them. He wouldn't tell them how they'd driven him to the force; he'd just let them off with a warning.

But he never pulled one of them over. Perhaps they were cautious drivers. He'd pulled his own mother over once, which was embarrassing for everyone. This time, this night, though, sometime around three in the morning, he pulled over a weaving car driven by (the license said) Bernard Feldstein.

Cottinend police rode with partners only on alternating weeks, and this week Oberman was alone. It was a very dark night on Rano Boulevard. The lawns all sported skeletons and inflatable black cats. This Bernard Feldstein's face was sunken and haunted.

"You look like you've seen a ghost," said Officer Oberman.

"I've seen a spook," the young man mumbled back automatically.

But when he got out of the car to walk a straight line and take a breathalyzer: The young man was completely sober.

"I'm fine," said Mr. Feldstein. "I was just thinking."

"About the ghost?"

"Yeah. About the spook."

He did not appear to be on drugs. Oberman let him off with a warning.

They never met again.

7 The next day, on the way home from work, Colin Lang bought a white board. He made his notes in marker, and erased them immediately afterwards. ¶ The most important part was to avoid any record of anything. Colin considered burning the napkin Bernie had given him, but he was afraid he would forget the address. It was on a dead-end side street, so he could hardly drive past and memorize the house, and an address might prove a hard thing to remember over the long, upcoming months. He folded the napkin in half and hid it in the pantry under a can of mixed nuts. It would be less damning than writing it down himself.

Any research he had to do he did from the library computer. There was a lot of research, most of it innocent on the face; anything too compromising he skipped. At the beginning of the plan there was room to "wing it"; only the end must be worked out thoroughly. He cleared the library computer's bowser history after each session. To conceal why he had come to the library in the first place, he checked out a book from the fiction section he was not going to read, one old enough that he could look up a plot summary easily in case the librarian asked him, when he returned it, how he had enjoyed *Nicholas Nickleby*.

He started using the exercise bikes at the gym.

An old physical White Pages—the original untraceable search—confirmed Bernard Feldstein's address. Coronet Street, as he said. It wasn't a total blow-off, then.

On November first, Colin stopped shaving. He told his boss he was raising awareness for men's health, and he passed around the office fliers for the Movember Foundation, with suggestions on how to make a donation. His face itched terribly.

At a thrift store he bought a plaid shirt, a cotton scarf, and two mesh baseball caps, one of which read CAT across the front. At a hardware store—one a half-day's weekend journey north—he bought two pairs of black painter's coveralls, special ones with two zippers. At a sporting goods store he bought a gym bag, one made for a lacrosse stick.

"Kids," he said, rolling his eyes when the clerk rang the bag up. *You know kids and their lacrosse games,* he tried to imply. "Am I right?" Always he paid cash.

He put the clothes and gym bag into a drawer in his bedroom, a drawer he first cleaned out very carefully, with Windex and paper towels, so there was nothing touching the cloth but antiseptic Ikea pasteboard. The gym bag, plaid shirt, and CAT cap were on top. He'd need them first.

Colin knew Blande Boulevard because it was one way of getting to I-81. His mother was in a retirement home in Salton, fifty minutes north on I-81, and if Blande was not the most convenient route to the onramp from Colin's house, it made for a handy alternate. He started driving up and down Blande after work. There was a four-mile stretch, between Maple Street and the access roads to the I-81 ramps, where Blande Boulevard had no cross streets, no exits, no escape. There was a scenic median, but it was protected by low metal railings. Right beyond the breakdown lane, on either side, grew tangled tree cover.

Traffic was the most important consideration, and he'd never get an accurate idea of traffic patterns from weekend, or nighttime, excursions; so he called out one day from work ("dentist's appointment") and drove up and down Blande in rush hour. It would not do to get caught in stopped traffic when the day came, but he noticed that northbound traffic lightened to a trickle after nine, while southbound traffic still came quick and regular.

In daylight, for this was the first time he had been on Blande Boulevard before sundown in quite some time, he spied a brief break in the in the northbound side's tree cover. An overgrown dirt road, visible now merely as tall grass and fern between the spaced-out trees, snaked into the forest. Colin only spotted it as he was already zooming past, so he looped all the way around and on his next pass pulled over into the breakdown lane. He got out of the car and trudged through the brush. The road, or trail, curved behind some trees and ended in what must have once, years ago, been a maintenance shed, now a pile of corrugated rust. Hiking a little past, Colin found a steep embankment overlooking the rear parking lot of Choice Pizza on Route 434. Climbing up from the parking lot might be difficult, though hardly impossible, but sliding down the grassy slope would be child's play.

Route 434—Ridgemont Road—did not connect to the highway. Colin had been to Choice Pizza, once, many years ago. It was at least a fifteen-minute drive from Blande Boulevard.

Colin hurried back to his car. Already a good samaritan had pulled over, and was loitering over the car, offering help. Colin waved the do-gooder away.

"I thought I saw a bobcat," he said, pointing his thumb towards the woods. "Turned out to be just a stray dog."

Perhaps it wasn't wise, to hop out of a car and chase a bobcat into the woods, but nature boys do stupid things, don't they? The samaritan drove away to antagonize someone else. Colin drove home. The completed plan appeared, fully formed, in his mind now, although he would have to write it on the white board again and again to work out the details.

8 Nine days after the night at the Munster Pub, a Sunday, Colin drove to Pennsylvania to get his rifle. The Pennsylvania state line was only half an hour away from Cottinend, New York, but the gun show was six hours west of

that. Colin left before dawn. He had a money belt full of really a lot of cash tucked into the waistband of his jeans. He was wearing the plaid shirt he'd bought, with an old gray sweatshirt over it. With the CAT baseball cap pulled low over his eyes, and his week's worth of November beard, he looked nothing like Colin Lang, F. S. A.: Fellow of the Society of Actuaries, that is. The gym bag was in the back seat. His cell phone he'd left at home, of course. There would be no record. He was taking no risks.

Shoreditch, Pennsylvania, was far from the highway and not easy to find, especially for someone who had grown accustomed to his phone's GPS. The gun show was in the ballroom of their Elks Club hall, and shared space with a *poison fair*, so-called. Colin walked through the door with his gym bag and found himself faced with cage after cage of venomous snakes. One table had terraria of scorpions and centipedes. Curious shoppers milled around and made it hard to squeeze between them. Colin couldn't stop scratching his neck.

"Am I in the wrong place?" Colin said, perhaps out loud.

"You want to buy a bat?" an old woman in a powder blue track suit asked Colin. She was standing behind some scorpions.

"A bat?"

"They're not poison, you know. They're like kittens."

"A rifle?" Colin asked, and the woman glumly pointed, with an arm hidden by dozens of Easter-colored hard plastic bracelets, to the other side of the ballroom. Colin dodged through a labyrinth of booths and cages and women in bathing suits with albino pythons draped over their shoulders to emerge among a new tangle of vendors, each with rack after rack of shotguns and pistols and rifles. Some of them were also selling, or at least displaying, tarantulas.

The whole atmosphere was so far outside Colin's daily experience—even the echoing from the high-ceiling was a sound he hadn't heard since some job fair in college. He felt conspicuous in his dress, like a man parodying the outfits of the people around him. Indeed, he was. How did you even ask to buy a gun? How did you do the thing you'd never done before? In his left front pants pocket rested a Swiss army knife, but that appeared to make him the least well-armed man in the building.

His heart began to jackhammer, but then Colin remembered: he was dead inside. If something as simple as a room full of firearms and vipers was going to get him all excited, there was hardly any point in going through with the plan.

How did you do the thing you'd never done before? Now *that*, indeed, was the question that next April was designed to answer. Colin strode somewhat purposefully up to a vendor. The man was wearing a khaki vest that was full of pockets, and every pocket full. His beard was fuller than Colin's. He stood behind a plastic folding table piled high with boxes of ammunition. Behind him was a pegboard partition festooned with rifles.

"Hello," Colin said. "I'm interested in an automatic rifle."

"A semi automatic?" the man asked.

"An automatic," Colin repeated, and the man began laughing.

"How many thousands of dollars do you have?" he choked out between his obvious and fake guffaws.

Colin was taken aback. Certainly he shouldn't reveal how much money he had stashed on his person. "A couple?" he said.

"Yeah, that'll get you sweet Fanny Adams. An automatic rifle! Glorious Christ!"

"I was under the impression," Colin said primly—he tried to remember the old Colin, the bad Colin who had spent two teenaged hours in a holding cell with pimps and junkies and possibly (who knew?) murderers; he tried to remember how that self-styled rebel would talk—"that everything was legal here. I wouldn't want to break the law." Not the best impression.

"Bully for you. Look, you want an assault rifle?"

Colin certainly did! It turned out that automatic weapons were perhaps technically legal but so heavily regulated that it even if the cost were not prohibitive, the *government attention* required to buy one would be. It turned out what Colin wanted was a semiautomatic tricked out with a bump stock to make it approximate the action of an automatic.

"Like an M-16," the seller claimed.

"Like a firehose?" Colin asked.

"No, like an M-16."

Colin wished he knew if this was true, if bump stocks worked. His library research had really been restricted to questions on what states had the laxest gun laws and where the nearest gun shows were—the locations of Halloween stores and abandoned campgrounds—maps of Cottinend—anodyne questions that weren't even suspicious. He'd never thought to ask Google "how do you make an only very deadly gun very very deadly without attracting ATF attention?" His knowledge of firearms, frankly, came mostly from action movies he'd stopped watching as a teenager.

But semi-automatic or bump stock notwithstanding, what Colin really wanted, what he *really wanted* was for no one to card him or record his name anywhere. He was prepared to walk away from the sale if the man asked for ID; but this turned out not to be necessary.

"I'll also need a lot of ammunition," Colin said, "and...some of those." He pointed at the magazines. "The long ones."

"Sure. I'm supposed to ask you what you're buying this for," the vendor said. "Hunting, home security..."

"Oh, that's easy," said Colin. "I'm trying to impress a girl."

And the vendor nodded as though this was the most natural thing in the world.

9 It was a long drive back to Cottinend, but Colin had a couple of stops to make. He took an exit to a small town with a sad little Halloween popup store, one of the places he'd looked up at the library. *Everything up to 75% off,* said the signs. The poor store couldn't last too much longer into November; doubtless a Christmas shop would spring up in another week or two.

Colin parallel parked at a meter, and left his firepower in the gym bag in the backseat. He'd had a hard time closing the zipper over the long rifle, which made him wonder if he'd actually bought a lacrosse-sized gym bag after all. He locked the car, even though there was no one in sight, no other cars on the street. He had a two-grand investment in that bag. One quarter for the meter, and he tingalinged the door of the shop.

He picked out two Alfred E. Neuman masks, one blonde pageboy wig, and a junior disguise kit, with nose putty and cheek cotton and fake facial hair.

A chain-smoking high school girl was behind the counter. "Why are you buying two masks and only one wig?" she asked.

Colin's first instinct was to respond, "Is everybody in this state an asshole?" but he bit it back. There was no reason to highlight the fact that he was from New York. There was no reason to be memorable. He could have shut her up, of course; he could have gone to the car, come back in with his purchase held casually over one arm. She would have minded her own business then.

But he just said, "Twins, am I right?" and paid cash. The door dinged on the way out. By the time he needed a disguise, by the time he used anything he'd bought, this shop would be out of business. Even if the products were traced back to this place, even if someone somehow managed to find what seasonal workers had killed their time working here—why would this girl remember this boring scruffy man in plaid? He walked back to his car, almost whistling. He didn't whistle.

His next stop was a campground that the internet claimed had closed a full month ago. Up to this moment he had broken no laws. He was a law-abiding actuary. Owning a bump stock in Pennsylvania was still legal back then. Driving around with a rifle in the backseat was an innocent pastime. The Alfred E. Neuman masks were nothing but an eccentricity. His next move—he had no idea if it was legal, but he assumed it would be low risk. He parked in the empty lot and walked down a path into the woods, his gym bag under his arm. There were still several hours of daylight left, and although the trees were dense overhead, most of the limbs were already bare; the sun filtered down leaving crazy, spindly shadows. Some tree trunks were blazed with blue swatches of paint.

Colin Lang had never fired a gun before. He knew the basics: which end to point away from you. The bearded vendor had gone over the intricacies of loading and had even installed the bump stock using an Allen wrench on a multitool he kept clipped to his kilt. When Colin decided he was isolated enough, he stopped and filled one, two, three magazines, one bullet at a time. Then he checked that the safety was on. He pushed a magazine into the rifle. It failed to snap in place, so Colin turned it around; this time it went home.

Taking careful aim at a nearby tree, Colin pulled the trigger. Nothing happened. He flipped the safety off, aimed, and pulled the trigger again. The gun bucked like a cat and flew out of Colin's hands. It was as loud as the Fourth of July; it was like trying to hold a skyrocket. There was more smoke than he'd imagined. There was more everything than he'd imagined.

Colin picked the rifle up, aimed and tried again. The bumpstock really worked! He just held the trigger and the gun kept up a rapid-fire. It took only a moment to go through a whole magazine of bullets, forty rounds. Colin took out another magazine. He didn't have to be a good shot. He just needed to be able to hold it steady.

The sky was darkening when Colin turned back and followed the blue swatches back to his car. He climbed in and after a few false starts found his way back to the interstate. He held one of the Neuman masks on his lap: it was a rubbery mask that you pulled all the way over your head like a ski mask. He waited until night had good and fallen; he waited until there was a long straightaway and no other cars in sight. Holding the steering wheel steady with his knees he slipped the mask on. It wobbled and caught and took longer to pull into place than he had anticipated. The car swerved precipitously. The mask's eyeholes were small and ruined his peripheral vision; the slit at the mouth was small, and the mask soon filled up with his stifling, stale breath. Colin pulled over to the side of the highway, put on his hazards, and cut the eyeholes larger with his jack-knife. He enlarged the hole at the mouth.

"Maybe I should have bought more than two masks, in case I screw this up," he said in the black, stifling silence of the car. He put the mask on and began to drive again. Better; he could see better.

Both masks were mutilated but serviceable by the time he reached home. The lights he'd turned on that morning were still on. He slipped the car into the garage. He selected some DVDs he'd watched a dozen times before and set them by the television. If anyone asked he'd say he spent the day watching movies.

No one asked.

10 Officer John Oberman crouched behind the vehicle in the synagogue parking lot and watched the three boys and wondered: How much of a swastika did he have to let them paint?

The easiest thing to do would be to allow them to finish their graffiti, however many swastikas and slurs and swear words they wanted to produce. Then he could nab them as they came back to their vehicle. He'd already popped the hood —they hadn't even locked the car—and removed the starter relay. They weren't going anywhere.

But then the synagogue would be covered in swastikas! Someone would have to clean off the graffiti, and cleaning just one swastika was hard enough. Maybe he should go as soon as they started, walk right up and arrest them. Even if they bolted, they'd be leaving the car there; it's not like he wouldn't know who they were. If he did it this way, he wouldn't even have to explain away the starter relay in his pocket; taking it from a car was not strictly legal, even though he did it all the time. It was his signature trick. He called it his trademark.

"You've got to wait," his partner whispered between expectorations. Campbell was sitting spread-legged, leaning against the tire. He couldn't smoke here, lest the smoke give him away, so he chewed, aiming the juice so it landed right between his shoes. It did not always land right between his shoes. He was watching Oberman with his one good eye, and perhaps he could tell that he was about to run forward.

"They'll jack up the synagogue," Oberman said.

"You're just worried about the relay," Campbell said. "Put it back and no one will know."

"I'm not worried about the relay; I'm worried about the synagogue."

Campbell spat. It ricocheted off the tip of his shoe. Shoes like these were no longer required as part of the uniform, but Campbell was old enough that he wore them anyway, while also being slovenly enough that he would coat them in tobacco juice. "If you go now, what do you have them for? Planning a hate crime by text?"

"Social media isn't texting," Oberman said, not for the first time.

"Whatever. It's all computer bullshit. It's all" (Campbell warmed up to the subject) "*cyber* bullshit." He then said *cyber bullshit*, or the equivalent, six or seven more times.

The three boys—Pelilla, Carter, and Parkhurst—had been called in by a suspicious hardware store clerk after buying spray paint with what the clerk though, in retrospect, might be a fake ID. Turned out to be Pelilla's older brother's real ID, but in a routine check before he did anything, Oberman had found on Parkhurst's Twitter (back then it was still Twitter) feed…this threat, this synagogue.

Campbell would not let it go. "Internet bullshit." He never returned to the actual topic—rush them now or wait—but Oberman understood: Let the kids commit a serious crime before you arrest them. Otherwise what are you even arresting them for?

So the two of them lurked in the darkened parking lot, waiting for three teenage idiots to ruin their lives.

11 When Colin thought about it in general terms, as opposed to specific, step-by-step terms, he called it, in his head, the Incident. ¶ The Incident was a ways away. It was nearly six long months until April. When Colin Lang had told

Bernie *April*, hadn't he picked the date at random? He'd looked at a calendar on his phone, but it just been a random work day, or rather the night before a random work day. But hadn't he also been putting the Incident off as long as possible? Assigning the actual job not to him, but whatever future-Lang would be in existence six months from then?

Nevertheless, the April date (Colin figured) had been fortuitous. He needed time for everyone at Munster to forget his face. He needed time for the poison fair/gun show to forget that gawky rube from the north. He needed the leaves to come in on the trees.

Colin wiped every part of the rifle down with a disinfectant wipe. He tried wiping the gym bag down, but decided he didn't know how, and just went out and bought another one, being careful not to touch it without gloves. (The encroaching winter made it easier to wear gloves in the store.) This time he went further out of town, to a small sporting good store in Pennsylvania. He bought, while he was there, a dark gray windbreaker with a hood and a pair of hiking boots, making sure to select a brand and size he'd worn before. He didn't try them on. They turned out to be too large to fit into the bedroom drawer, so he tucked the boots in the basement, where they didn't even look out of place.

The old gym bag went in the garbage, as did the plaid shirt and the CAT cap. Nothing wrong with throwing out old clothes. Nothing wrong with a windbreaker in a drawer or boots in a basement. Colin wasn't even a criminal, really. A rifle like this was probably illegal in New York, but he put it in his basement, in the gym bag, half-inside (it stuck out) a suitcase in a closet near the boiler room; if anyone actually found it there, he could always plead ignorance of the complicated patchwork of firearms regulations that made up the American landscape.

Back when he had been studying for his actuarial exams, Colin had figured out a secret that let him sail through them while so many of his peers had had to retake test after test. The secret was: Never stop thinking about the actuarial exams. While you were driving, while you were shopping at the supermarket, think about actuarial math. While you were showering, while you were kissing a girl, think about mortality in cohorts. Never stop. This went on for years.

Once the exams had finished, Colin had nothing to think about. But now he thought about the plan. He drew diagrams on the white board, he wrote checklists on the white board, and every night he erased them all. The great day was still a long way off, and Colin found this comforting. He ran every event over and over in his head, and he had so many times left to do it. He had so many days of nothing but him and the plan. Everything was easy except not getting caught, and not getting caught would be very tricky.

The key was how quickly the rifle fired. He could run through an entire magazine in three seconds. How many cars could he reasonably be expected to pass in three seconds? He would have to take out one magazine and snap in another quickly. There was no way to practice the actual firing—bringing the rifle out of the house was too dangerous—but he could practice switching magazines. He owned a pair of tight leather driving gloves, and they made his fingers feel thick. When he practiced while wearing them, he bobbled and dropped more magazines than he got in place. For one wild moment, Colin feared that a gloved finger would not be able to fit into the trigger guard, but when he triple checked to make sure the gun was unloaded, double checked the safety, and slipped his finger around the trigger, there was plenty of room. He tried flexing his index finger—not directly on the trigger, but around it, near it—and it felt fine.

Night after night, after work, in the basement, he got better at switching magazines rapidly. He sat down cross-legged, leaning several magazines against his thighs; with a gloved hand he popped one free from the rifle, grabbed another off the floor and snapped it home. Eject, grab, repeat. Any action repeated again and again gets smoothed out, like a stone in a stream, and after a couple of weeks, Colin could replace a magazine in an eyeblink.

He returned *Nicholas Nickleby* to the library. No black marks on his record like an overdue fine! No librarian asked him about it.

There had been nothing suspicious about the time Colin spent on the library computer map of Cottinend. Who isn't interested in the local geography? Finally he decided, though, that he was better off with a paper map and after a few false starts found one at a gas station.

His beard stopped itching. Because he could not shave at all, by the Movember rules he had laid out and passed around work, it came in uneven, and his neck looked ridiculous. People at work gave him the ironic thumbs up, but Colin was thinking about the plan. He could hardly lean a series of magazines against his thighs in a moving car. This was the riddle.

In search of an answer, Colin stalked in the evenings through department stores and Salvation Army centers. He had no idea what he was looking for; the instinct of a lifetime told him that a product would be the answer to his problem, and he just had to find out what it was. His patchy beard, which he was already regretting, made him feel conspicuous, so he left his coat in the car; since he came from work, he was wearing a nicely tailored suit. It would hardly do for the police to pick him up as a vagrant.

He passed other dead souls wandering the aisles, their eyes scanning shelves blankly for an answer that never came. He wanted to tell them that he was not like them, not any more. But he didn't say a word.

No one knew anything. He could back out at any time. He would never back out.

12 Delia Jancewicz frogmarched Alan, her only son, to the car. He would be upset if they were late, even by a minute, but he also refused to hurry. He took his time tying his shoes; he took his time buttoning and rebuttoning his jacket. Years ago Delia could just pick him up and bodily set him in the car, but Alan was now twenty-eight. She marched him along, holding both his elbows behind his back—somewhat gently with the hand that held the keys. She had pushed the keys into his flesh once, quite by accident, and the deep impression the teeth left on his upper arm had turned blue and lasted for days.

23

Alan only slowly pulled one foot and then the other deliberately into the car. But his eye, Delia could tell, was on the time. They had to pass the mailbox while the dashboard clock read 10:15. Alan didn't throw his tantrums much any more, but he could sulk, and a good sulk could ruin the day through dinnertime.

Delia always backed into the driveway when she came home so that they could exit driving forward. It was so much easier to pull into the street driving forward, and Alan seemed to prefer it, too. She passed the mailbox, yes, at quarter after, and they headed on their usual route.

"2013 Mazda MX-5," said Alan, visibly relaxing into his seat. They were on time. "2015 Honda Accord."

The constant patter could get on her nerves some days, but usually Delia valued this little routine. Alan was so mercurial most of the time, and small things set him off; but on their ride, she knew exactly what might trigger him: tardiness, too-light traffic, cardinals.

Alan, Delia knew, hated cardinals. As they drove past the park he kept his eyes away from its greenery, and across his mother, out the driver's side window. This is where the cars were, anyway. In his youth, Alan used to write down the cars he saw, but this proved time consuming. He tried preparing checklists, but flipping through all those pages took even more time than jotting anything down. He seemed to have mellowed with age, satisfied now just to acknowledge the plenty, the myriad of cars that zoomed by. It was the pleasure of mastery; he named models of cars Delia had never even heard of. Or at least he did sometimes; their routine ensured that they passed few strange cars. There were not a lot of out-of-towners in Cottinend. The same Grand Cherokees and Lexuses repeated again and again.

But that day, Alan said something different that started Delia from her reverie. "What was that?" Delia asked him.

"I said, 'He was smiling again.' It's been weeks, he's always smiling. He never smiled."

"Who, honey?" Delia asked.

And a look came over Alan's face that Delia might have called cagey if she could have been more certain of her angle of view. Her eyes were primarily on the road, of course.

"The 1983 Mercury Zephyr," Alan answered.

13
People kept saying to Bernie, "What's wrong with you?" People had always said that to Bernie, sometimes in a friendly fashion, after he'd told a dirty joke, but usually angrily, after he'd screwed something up. But now it seemed more or less like an honest question.

Bernie just smiled and nodded and kept his mouth shut.

At times it seemed like he'd dreamed the whole encounter—the well-dressed stranger with hair severely parted. Theodore. But then he'd look at the piece of paper he'd stuck to the refrigerator: April 10.

"Hey, Nardo!" Stone yelled when he was getting a beer from the fridge. Jason Stone used to come over to play Bernie's Xbox and steal his beer. "What happens April 10?"

"Got a date," Bernie said cautiously from the couch.

By the time Stone had walked back into the living room the beer can was empty. He was already turning around to the kitchen again. "It's still my turn," he said. "And seriously, what's in April? Parole hearing? AIDS test?"

All Bernie had to do was tell one person about his—what was it? glorious destiny. Stone's jaw would hit the floor. Stone's head would spin around. He'd never make fun of Bernie Feldstein again.

But instead Bernie just started laughing a long, relatively fake, contemptuous laugh.

"What's wrong with you?" asked Stone.

14
Colin drove to his mother's assisted-living retirement community for Thanksgiving. He took Blande Boulevard to I-81, although the holiday traffic was anomalous enough that he did not treat the trip as providing data.

Sunset Grove served Thanksgiving dinner in a large dining room. The waiters were dressed as pilgrims, the waitresses as Wampanoags. The patrons and their guests dressed formally, or at least in a jacket and tie. Colin simply wore work clothes.

"You look like a bum," his mother said, patting, too vigorously to be comfortable, his hirsute cheek.

"I know," said Colin.

On November 29 he dropped a thousand-dollar donation at the Movember Foundation website. It was by far the largest charitable donation he had ever made, and probably the only one he had made without someone, a coworker or Cub Scout, asking him for it. On November 30 he shaved his beard.

15 Bernie's parents were both dead—that's how he had his own house, by squatting and then inheritance—and his brother was all the way in Hawaii, but his mother's sister and her husband lived two towns over. On Thanksgiving he headed there, missing like an absent lover his daily drive on Blande Boulevard. Even weekends, now, he hated—he so longed for the trip down Blande, the momentary glimpse of that bulbous freak Jancewicz, soon to die. To miss it on a Thursday, a weekday, was depressing enough, but that Thursday, to make it worse, he also had to see Aunt Janice and Uncle Stan. If his cousins were there, he'd just turn around and go home.

His cousins were there—they lived nearby, of course—and yet Bernie did not go home. Stan Jr. and Maggie were treating him differently, right off the bat.

"Have you been working out, Bernard?" Stan Jr. asked. If he didn't ask it exactly, he *implied* it.

Everyone else was wearing a polo shirt or a sweater and Bernie was wearing a long-sleeved T with a photorealistic skull on it—perhaps a snake was slithering out of the eye socket, and perhaps this shirt, or one like it, had been a source of contention at previous family gatherings. But now Bernie perceived that he was in the right. Everyone else, with their twee outfits and eggnog-colored pants, had overdressed for the occasion.

"Did you lose weight?" asked Maggie.

Bernie played the strong silent type. He figured that just telling them the truth would shatter their worlds and their minds, irrevocably. Better to let them notice it gradually—his glorious destiny, his vast power.

"Because you look different."

Bernie ate heartily and got up to make coffee—everyone else in the Fine household drank tea, but they kept a can of instant for guests, and Bernie didn't even wait to be asked. He just got up and went to the kitchen. As the kettle reached a boil he thought about how his life had changed, and how it would just keep getting better. After April 10, the respect he received would blossom like (he actually thought this up) the flowers of spring.

When it came time to pour the hot water into the mug—the Fines' kettle must have been shaped differently from the one he had at home, and in canting his wrist to pour, the searing-hot metal of the kettle's side touched his forearm. Bernie's first instinct—half-accomplished—was to pull away, but then he thought twice. He let the kettle rest against his forearm, against the hairless fleshy part right above the elbow. It didn't even hurt that much, really, not someone like Bernie. Could a normal man do this?

He came back into the dining room proudly carrying a coffee mug with a red blistering arm, the skin already starting to slough off.

"Bernard! What happened to you?"

Stan Jr. shook his head. "He always was retarded."

16 Right before Christmas, like a miracle, Colin found what he needed at a Target. He'd been there shopping for a bicycle—window shopping really, since he wasn't going to buy anything until the post-Christmas sales. He wore his gloves, just in case, as he walked through the store, but this was not so

unusual late in the year. On his way out he passed, by chance, an endcap: GREAT GIFTS FOR DAD!!

"Why," he said, perhaps out loud, "do they even make these any more?" But there between the novelty painted tie and the smokeless indoor grill was a plastic spring-loaded VHS tape holder. Colin was about to buy three or five, but then decided this would be suspicious, so he bought one.

"Fathers, am I right?" he said to the clerk. He paid, just in case, cash.

Once at home, in his basement, coat off but gloves on, he unboxed the tape holder. It was a simple device, just two flat plastic plates, translucent and powder blue, connected by three plastic rods. The pates were pressed close together by spring action, but you could pull them apart easily, and set a tape between them. The three rods would make a sort of cradle for the tape, and then the whole con-traption could sit on a shelf. Since VHS tapes stood up on a shelf easily on their own, it seemed like a worthless device for the average dad—not to say an anachronism by a good decade or two—but it offered a solution for Colin.

He set seven magazines in the tape holder, which was as many as he could fit. The spring held the magazines tightly in place. He pulled one magazine out, and all six others came out with it, clattering across the cement floor. He packed them in again, and tried removing one magazine by tipping it forward and then snap-ping it out quickly. This worked better; one magazine came out, and the spring contracted to hold the other six. After a few more trials he found he could reliably remove a magazine by first adjusting it into place—bent forward so it was almost perpendicular to the other magazines—and then snapping it free.

He practiced late into the night. He was beginning to master a technique of flicking the top of the magazine, so it would rotate into the correct position, and he could grab it loose in one motion. It got easier the shorter the tape holder grew —the fewer magazines that were in it, that is—so that pulling one free when there were only two or three magazines left was a simple matter.

The last lone piece, though, was hard. He tried holding the magazine and flicking his wrist so that the tape holder shot off, leaving the magazine in his hand. The cheap plastic holder flew across the basement landing with a crack against the hard floor before skidding away into the shadows. He heard a second crack as it hit the wall.

Colin was up in a shot. He raced over to the wall, but his body blocked the light and he couldn't see what shape the tape holder was in. When he stepped to one side, only then could he confirm that the tape holder was in one piece. He brought it into the light, and there on the powder blue sides was a crisscross of cracks.

He smeared super glue all over the side and went to bed. Get a few hours of sleep before work. It was only the Christmas party, after all.

But on the way to work he put on nose putty, a fake mustache, and a wad of padding under his upper lip that gave him a permanent sneer. Back (and not for the last time) to Target, just as it opened. He stashed the spare tape holder in his trunk and removed his disguise at a red light. He wasn't even dressed like himself, so that was one thing. It was a Christmas party, and he had on a horrible sweater his mother had made him.

17 Carol Wernick had been working at Radcliffe Worth Partners for a little less than six months. She'd grown up only twenty miles from Cottinend, and had thought that moving back to the area after four years at Amherst College would have given her a support network of friends she could fall into; but her network, dispersed for college, had not reformed. No one else had come home to stay. One lived in Poughkeepsie now, the rest in the New York City area, and only Carol had ended up half a mile from her childhood home, working, in the years before Radcliffe Worth, for IBM.

Carol had never made friends easily, and all that time at the IBM actuarial department she'd been studying for her exams instead of socializing. By the time exams were done, she had acquired a reputation for being aloof or square—she wasn't sure which—and the people she saw every day were stuck as mere acquaintances. Her parents were her only social outlet—this was square, to be sure, but she'd been forced into it. She started looking for another job not because she didn't like it at IBM but just because she thought being the "new girl" somewhere might help her be social.

Her plan had been to get a job in the City, or even Albany, but Radcliffe Worth in Cottinend had made an offer, and they were only two towns over. Technically she didn't even have to pack up her house and move (although she did, just to get a better commute and make it feel like a fresh start).

The first few months at her new job she'd tried to be friendly to everyone, but she began to think the problem wasn't that she wasn't the "new girl." The problem was her. She'd been unfun for so long it was too late to be fun.

Sitting at her desk, trying to decide if she should put on lipstick for a mere office party, she made a promise to herself: "I am going to let my hair down. I am going to be fun, and I am going to have fun at this party. If I have to get drunk, I will get drunk." Carol's hair was too short to literally be let down, but she knew what she meant.

There were problems with her plan. The primary problem was that no one (she assumed) had ever had fun at an office Christmas party. There might be games. She had a small present of chocolates wrapped up for what had originally been called a Yankee swap before someone (*who? how?*) had decided the word Yankee might be offensive (*how? to whom?*) and was now called a white elephant swap. She dreaded participating in a white elephant swap. It had been so long since she had received a gift from a non-family member that she wasn't sure she could ape the correct facial expressions while unwrapping one.

The break room stank of the oppressive loneliness of fake conviviality. Bartholomew Parnel, who had the cubicle across from hers, was loudly complaining, "Why is it that a worthless elephant has to be a *white* elephant? Does that sound right to you?" Carol swerved away from him. Ahead of her was Colin Lang.

Carol had never before spoken to Colin Lang, but he seemed like a natural choice to approach. Before the November beard she'd barely noticed him, but

30

that bout of celebrity made him someone everyone knew. Talking to someone she didn't know was the whole point of this exercise, but difficult; talking to someone *everyone* knew was halfway there. With the ridiculous beard off, Carol thought, he even looked handsome in a way.

"I don't think I've been to a party like this since college," she said, after standing next to Colin for a moment.

"Can't say I really partied in college," he answered. "My high school days got it all out of my system."

"You were wild in high school?"

"I'm not proud of it," Colin said, watching her face (she noticed) from the corners of his eyes, "but my junior year I stole a cop car."

18 Bernie's bandage fell off one morning on the drive to work. Yes, the Fines had hurried him to the hospital, but all the understaffed, holiday-glum nurses had done was slap on some salve and a bandage. Bernie could have done that himself! He held his arm outside the shower every morning, and it took a full month for the medical tape to flap loose. That's how careful Bernie had been.

The skin underneath the bandage was white and puckered. With the bandage off, the smell of the unwashed flesh began to fill the poorly ventilated car. It smelled like the white flowers on the trees outside the pizza parlor. It made him think of spring.

19 There had been a time—many years ago—when Colin had tried. And when he tried, he had generally been successful. ¶ The cop car story, stealing a cop car—this youthful indiscretion was his cocktail party staple, and it was always a hit. His respectable facade was armor enough against any possibility that by this admission he had gone "too far." It was so long ago! He was a button-down solid citizen. But as far as crazy pasts went, a high speed-chase in a stolen cop car could usually trump the party. Anything worse and you simply couldn't joke about it. Anything worse was a tragedy.

31

Raise a glass to Colin Lang! He was well-dressed and owned his own house, and back when he was trying he found it easy to get a date by means of this story. He found it easy to get his dates to come to his house for a nightcap.

At first there was nothing weird about the house. He had no pictures on the walls, but who knew, maybe he had just moved in. Maybe he had just had it painted. Dates gave him the benefit of the doubt. Only later did it seem creepy. Only later did the deadness behind his eyes drift to the font of his eyes; or perhaps the eyes just became pellucid enough that you could see it through them.

He had not used the story in years, but when Carol started talking to him it had slipped out. They exchanged phone numbers, and on Christmas he sent her a friendly text. He was on his way, he explained, to his mother's. Have a great holiday.

It had been years since he tried, and he honestly wasn't really trying now. It was all autopilot. He was thinking about the plan.

20 Someone had called in a tip, but it was just a "worry-tip," and those were low priority. It eventually got passed to John Oberman, which was ridiculous—this was a job for a detective, not a patrolman.

"You like this nerd shit," Detective Smith said with a giggle. He dropped the paper on Oberman's desk. He left, still giggling; he had a movie giggle, Oberman thought, like a supervillain.

It was a printout of two related tweets that a certain @CottinendKing had produced a week prior, on New Year's Day. The first read: "next yer u will see how powrfull i am when i kil u all". The second: "i ment this yer sory". The tweets did not make a thread but presumably they were supposed to.

This was not even his job, but Oberman took out his phone, opened the Twitter app, and looked up @CottinendKing. The account did not post very much, and when it did it was mostly about wrestling. It had zero followers.

"Who called this in?" he yelled over to Smith.

As they drove around on patrol, Campbell just pooh-poohed the tweets. "There have to be a million Cottinends in America. How do you know this guy is even the king of *this* Cottinend."

"There are absolutely not a million Cottinends in America. This is actually the only Cottinend in the whole world."

Campbell kept trying to light his cigarette, but this was hard to do one-handed with a greasy old matchbook while driving. Theoretically, Campbell could do it, as he had done it before; but he was not doing it today. The cigarette bobbled in his lips wildly as he said, "How could you possibly know that?"

"'Kill you all,'" Oberman said. "How is this guy going to kill us all?"

"He's not literally the King of Cottinend, I'll tell you that much."

21 So many boxes got recycled in the weeks after Christmas, surely no one would notice several boxes for VHS tape holders, disassembled, turned inside out and pressed flat.

It was ice cold out, but Colin started biking. He'd go for a quick ride before work, when it was still dark. If he unsnapped two levers and took the front wheel off, he found, his new bike could fit in his back seat, but he didn't actually bother driving it anywhere. He just rode around the neighborhood. It's like they said: you never forget. But his leg muscles had been dormant since junior high, and although he'd tried to build them back up with the stationary bike at the gym, it turned out that the a gym bike wasn't quite the same as a ride up and down hills. It might take a while before he felt could ride for any length of time easily.

He'd expected to do most of his biking on the weekend—the plan called for biking on the weekend—but there was a monkey wrench in the plan. It was a weekend wrench, now. Its name was Carol Wernick.

I hear him, and shake hands with him; and we talk, and walk, and dine, and so on; but I don't believe it. Nothing is real.
•Dickens, *David Copperfield* (1850)..

II. A Nice Place to Visit.

Colin Lang • Carol Wernick • John Oberman • The Sp!der • Alan Jancewicz • Bernie Feldstein • Cottinend, N.Y. • Colin Lang • Bernie Feldstein • The Sp!der • Carol Wernick • Colin Lang • Bernie Feldstein • Colin Lang • Carol Wernick • The Sp!der • Colin Lang • Carol Wernick • John Oberman • Bernie Feldstein • Carol Wernick

1 In retrospect, it certainly looked like the greatest risk Colin Lang had taken— the greatest risk he'd taken in decades, in fact—was suggesting a stranger might assist him in murder. This was the kind of thing you always ask yourself when you read it in the papers—"Wife Slain by Husband, Mistress"—*who brought it up*? Who said, "Baby, I love you, and now we have to kill (my / your) wife"?

Few people would call Colin audacious, but he had husbanded his audacity— a rainy day fund, perhaps. He understood, as an actuary, risk. Inviting your mistress to a murder was a high risk, in the sense that she might leave in a huff; she might turn you in for *attempted conspiracy*. This Bernard Feldstein—what was he going to do in a huff? For the first week after they met, Colin's most suspicious activity had been buying a purchasing board or showing a newfound fondness for Dickens. If the cops were going to come, they'd've come before he'd done anything even slightly dodgy. It wasn't much of a risk.

He sat on his living room couch, thinking, as he so often did. The early morning sun was coming through the bay window, lighting up a thin white curtain. He was thinking about the plan. Somewhere along the line he'd decided that, given the sunk costs of his Christmas text, it would look less suspicious if he asked Carol out for a New Year's Eve at some local "watering hole" (as he'd called it) than if he'd ghosted her. It would have been suspicious, surely, if he'd looked too preoccupied to kiss her at midnight. Everything had flowed naturally over the next few weeks, and here it was the middle of January and he hadn't even had time to look up what streets in Cottinend had garbage pickup on Wednesday. There was so much to do and he hadn't been doing it.

Was this, he wondered, the actual risk? Bringing a relative stranger into his house, again and again, a distraction, just as he should be focusing on the upcoming Incident?

To the side he heard a footstep on the stair. "Oh, there you are," said Carol.

"I was just about to make us coffee," he said.

2 He was gone when she woke up that morning, but it was, of course his house. He could hardly be sneaking away. She rolled out of bed and dressed in the essentials—no socks, no bra. The bedroom was spare, to be sure, she thought. There was a photo of his mother (he'd explained) on the dresser, and that was the only decoration. She walked over and picked up the photo, as one does. Then she looked over her shoulder. It was just so weird, to own so little. But then Colin was weird. When she looked at him, it was clear, always, that he was thinking of something, something profound or (she groped for the word) *essential*. It made other men look trivial, or childish.

She was still looking over her shoulder as she put the photo down. Only after she had opened a drawer, by touch and at random, did she turn back to see what she'd revealed. It was a collection of boxers, so she closed the drawer as quickly as she could without slamming it. She wasn't looking to be a pervert.

Nevertheless, she tried another drawer, and another. A collection of folded sweaters meant nothing, even when she ran her hands underneath them to see if they hid a secret stash of weed or pornography. But the next drawer…

It was almost empty, but there inside were—she had to flop it over to see—one, no two identical black zippered denim coveralls, neatly folded. They looked unlike anything Colin would ever wear, and Carol could not resist picking them up. There was more underneath—a dark, plaid scarf and a blue baseball cap. They looked unworn.

There was something so uncharacteristic about the drawer that it felt almost obscene. And yet if this was Colin's terrible secret—could anything be more bland? Probably they were gifts, perhaps from an aunt, he had decided never to wear.

But...two pairs of coveralls?

Carol quickly refolded the coveralls, closed the drawer and, after a moment to compose herself, went to wander the house in search of its owner.

3 Every police who stayed on the job long enough got assigned a trademark. Take Davis: She had once come to a battery scene down by a sump; the perp had fled; she caught a bunch of mosquitos in a baggie and gave them to the detectives, encouraging them to have the bugs sampled for DNA. She figured that whoever the assailant was, his blood had to be in at least some of those mosquitos, and they could use the DNA to identify him. They'd just laughed at her. Maybe it was a stupid idea and maybe it was a good idea before its time. But after that everyone called her Bug Lady or Mosquito Girl or even (somewhat more cleverly) Skeeter Davis. That was her trademark forever.

John Oberman's trademark, he had always believed, had been removing the starter relays from suspicious vehicles so that persons of interest couldn't just hop in and drive away. First thing he did when he got a call was show up and start popping hoods. It was his signature move. But he was beginning to suspect that the other officers believed he had a different trademark.

"Did you find the computer killer yet?" Lepage asked Oberman in the coffee room. "I know you're obsessed with that hacker shit."

How could Oberman convince some of these dinosaurs that using the internet was, in fact distinct from hacking?

And here was the thing: Every week or so @CottinendKing would post something threatening. If Oberman really was into "hacker shit" or "cyber shit" or whatever they were accusing him of, maybe he'd know what to do about it.

"im blow up all this shit town body parts flin then whose sory huh" [sic].

37

"*Flin?*" Campbell asked when Oberman showed him his phone.

"*Flying*, I assume," said Oberman.

"You should know, you're the nerd shitlord," Campbell said, lighting a cigarette.

"How do you even know the word *shitlord*?" Oberman asked.

"I use Facebook, of course" Campbell sniffed.

Who was @CottinendKing? Oberman tried contacting Twitter, but they wanted a warrant before they'd do absolutely anything. He tried getting a warrant, but was told no.

"People trash talk on the Internet," Smith told him dismissively. "You of all people should know that."

"This guy could live in France for all we know," Police Chief Wanamaker explained. "There's zero reason to think it's our business, and less than zero to think it's your business." And a little later, a lot less kindly, "Get off your hobby horse, Oberman," the Chief said. "Just drop it."

But of course it wasn't his hobby horse. They just said it was his hobby horse, again and again, as though that made it true. His hobby horse was supposed to be starter relays.

"It's too vague," Campbell explained. "No one will do anything without a credible threat. This is just 'some time maybe in the future' blah blah."

The next day: "i comin for u pussyboy april 10" [sic].

Oberman lay in bed, not sleeping, although he was a man who needed a lot of sleep. He had always needed a lot of sleep. His girlfriend probably would have been sleeping, had Oberman's tossing let her.

"Tabitha," he said—and this, too, kept her from sleeping—"let's say there was a case..."

"You have cases now?"

"No. No, I mean hypothetically. If I thought a crime was being committed and everyone said there was no crime being committed..."

"Everyone like the judge?"

"No. No, I mean, like, say, a serial killer. If there were a couple of unsolved murders…"

Tabitha sat up. "There's a serial killer on the loose?"

"Honest, this is hypothetical. But say I see the connection between the murders…"

"A connection only you can see? Oh, Johnny." She lay back down and rolled over away from him.

"But it's just that everyone else blows it off."

"Don't be a jackass, Johnny, and go to sleep."

And of course he wanted to go to sleep. But instead he got up and brought his phone downstairs. And in the middle of the night, standing in his living room where no girlfriends could overhear, Oberman called the Sp!der.

4 Oberman didn't want to call the Sp!der, or course. No one wanted to call the Sp!der. Sp!der was a long talker, and all the time he had spent in his mother's basement, years and years now, with no one to talk to, had not curbed his garrulous tongue.

Sp!der's life was a series of texts and emails and forum posts, and, with the exception of his irritating mother, he usually never got to talk to anyone at all. Many of his so-called friends communicated entirely with gifs of celebrity reaction shots, and they expected Sp!der to do the same. So if Sp!der was going to get *on the phone* for once, of course he was going to milk this chance: Oberman knew this; Sp!der knew that Oberman knew this; which meant if Oberman was going to call him—especially in the wee hours of John Oberman's morning, for there was two hours' difference between Denver and Cottinend—he must have a good reason. Doubtless, Oberman wanted all this—*no texts, no emails* or he would have texted, he would have emailed—off the record. Doubtless, he was committing some crime.

"I will help you commit your crime," Sp!der said, in between breathless hot takes on several recent TV shows. Of course Sp!der was awake at this hour. The Sp!der never slept, at least not while his mother was sleeping.

"I'm not committing a crime," Oberman said. "I'm just looking for advice. Computer advice."

Sp!der had known Oberman back in high school, at a time when Oberman had not had very many friends. He'd helped Oberman with his math homework. That was back before junior year, when Sp!der's mother had left a messy family situation and taken young Sp!der, then known as Michael, to Colorado with her. They'd kept moderately in touch, John and Michael, as classmates will.

"You've come to the right place," said Sp!der. "In fact—"

"It's just Twitter. I'm trying to find who a guy is on Twitter."

"For a case?"

"Yeah, for a case."

"You're a detective now?"

"Look, I'm allowed to do research on cases. Probably. It's ambiguous some times. And the detectives think Twitter is some kind of video game. That's why I'm calling."

"And you don't even ask how I am," Sp!der sulked. But he was beaming. This was the most fun he'd had in weeks, and if he could make Oberman feel guilty about it, even better.

"Well, I—"

"You," said Sp!der, putting his feet up on a desk littered with empty Mountain Dew bottles, "must tell me everything; but first I will tell you *everything*."

5 Alan Jancewicz was part of a program with the official initials SPS. It was pronounced Sips, although Miss Gerri said it should really be pronounced Spes, because *spes* was another word for *hope*. Alan always called it SPS, all three initials, because he thought Sips sounded babyish and he had never heard any-one use the word *spes* to mean *hope*. He didn't believe *spes* was a real word.

His mother had signed him up. All the SPS participants went out to eat together on weekend afternoons, and once a month or so there'd be events—a circus, once, but mostly small events. A park, a dance recital.

This month they went to a marionette show. It was the story of Hansel and Gretel, a story Alan knew well; at least he had known it in his childhood. That was a long time ago! Alan had a hard time keeping his eyes on the stage, because he was fascinated by the way the marionettes hung, from wooden pegs, when they were not in use. He had once seen a cartoon of a man in a dungeon, hanging from manacles. The marionettes looked like that. Were they supposed to be alive or dead?

"Alan!" hissed Miss Gerri from behind him. "Pay attention!"

But he knew that he was in the middle of the row of seats. He knew Miss Gerri would not pull him out across everyone else to go yell at him in the lobby. The puppet show was dumb, anyway. Another moment of condescension in a life of condescensions. The gingerbread house was for babies.

Alan was used to being treated like a baby. His mother would tell anyone who listened that he was prone to temper tantrums. When his father got angry it was just anger, or maybe rage; only Alan had "tantrums." He still had to sleep with his door open. If he spent more than five minutes in the bathroom, his mother was banging on the door. If he rearranged the furniture in his room, his grumbling father pushed it back. He was not allowed to go on the internet unsupervised, even though the internet was full of cars. And other things.

There had been one incident on eBay with frogs, but that was seven years ago now. No need to hold it against him forever.

The only secrecies allowed in his life were the patterns of cars he saw out his window, or as he went for his daily drive. It was a secret because neither of his parents, nor even the neighbors that walked by smiling and waving, could understand these patterns. They could barely even recognize the relevant cars. *Buses and trucks. Two door vs. four door.* But Alan could see them all: Those optional tinted windows on the 2015 Nissan Altima. The slightly off-blink left turn signal of the 2008 Chevy Impala. One passed and then another passed, in a dance that was at once fairly predictable but continually surprising.

And this here one was only one extra secret among a thousand, a million: His old classmate, grinning in an ancient Zephyr. It meant nothing more or less than the van art on the vans, but some oddity made him think of it at off times. There was something about that grin.

Gretel was pushing the witch into the oven, but everyone could see that. Ignoring the clucking tongue of Miss Gerri, he stared at the tangled strings of the dangling woodcutter. The strings were not in fact tangled.

6 Bernie got caught smoking in the delivery van. Mr. Prishtine took him out to Pizza King's parking lot to yell at him, and since the parking lot was in front, every passing car got to see this small humiliation. If only Mr. Prishtine drove to work on Blande Boulevard! But Bernie had no idea where he lived.

Maybe he could find out. Maybe after he had already learned the ropes, Mr. Prishtine could be next on his list.

He had it out for Bernie, the old creep did, and really it was because Mr. Prishtine usually hired nothing but cute girls. His waitstaff all had giant boobs. Mr. Prishtine only put up with Bernie because Bernie did deliveries and was always out, where Mr. Prishtine didn't have to look at him.

Bernie went out for another delivery, cigarette behind his ear. He wanted to smoke again and blame the smell on the previous incident, but he didn't quite dare. What if he got fired and Mr. Theodore Anderson found out and the whole destiny plan got canceled? At a stoplight he pulled out his phone. Twitter app.

He typed: "pizza king sexist hat crime aganist ladie's mr..." but then he stopped because he had no idea how to spell "Prishtine." Then he worried if he posted it he'd get fired. Cars were honking. He drove with one hand and deleted the text with the other and wrote instead, "soon i will hav my regevne 1 by 1 u die" and didn't it mean the same thing?

Sic. It meant: Soon.

7 We should probably review. ¶ I-81 runs north–south, or northeast–southeast, for most of its path, but it's anomalously east–west where it cuts through Cottinend, dividing the town in two. North of the highway is the quaint, strollable Shopping District and the big office complexes; the southern half of town is more residential, and has the park—the one with the big playscape. In between the two halves is a lot of wild, empty, unused forest land, some of it swampy.

Technically, Cottinend is just a village, but it's *huge*, at least for New York. All that undeveloped land. It gets three exits on I-81, and one of them, the furthest east, is labeled simply BLANDE BLVD.

Blande snakes through Cottinend, connecting Hesitania (in the north) with Hobsons Falls. Between a sleepy development of raised ranches—Maple Street, Elm Street, and North and South Oak—and the ramps to I-81 lies the strip in question. Four miles of winding road, divided by a cultivated, fenced-in median (bright, in summer, with flowers). Very scenic. Forested on both sides. No exits.

No exits at all.

8 *Quietly competent* had been what Colin had always gone for, if he had gone for anything. "Competent and professional" is perhaps the phrase used earlier. He got good performance reviews, but nothing more. Nothing flashy.

But now the boss was calling him in for a special commendation. "You've just been so focused recently," Mr. Arnoux said from behind his big desk, shaking his head in good-natured disbelief. Colin recognized that there was some irony in this statement, as he had never, not once since he arrived at Radcliffe Worth, not even when his father died, been less focused on work.

"You're 'hitting it on all cylinders,'" Arnoux went on. He was fond of such phrases.

And certainly Colin was focused on *something*. He was focused on detail work.

There were still so many small details of the plan. Take the leather gloves. They kept Colin from leaving prints of course, but what if there were prints *on* them? He didn't anticipate forgetting the gloves at any crime scene, but something unexpected might happen. The soft inside would probably hold no prints, but the shiny outside? He could wipe them down, of course, but even putting them on would necessarily entail touching them again.

The gloves themselves were probably untraceable—Colin had owned them for so many years that even he didn't remember where they'd come from; and yet they were generic enough, just black leather, and could hardly be associated with him in anyone's minds. But the very age of the gloves increased the danger—how many hairs and skin cells were stuck in the lining? Could you...*wash* leather gloves? Would that work?

He could buy a new pair of gloves, but either he would have to practice with them on—in which case the hair and skin would build up in them as well—or he'd have to initiate the Incident with strange new gloves, never broken in. Certainly it would be foolish to try that!

All of these thoughts appeared and disappeared from the white board.

Finally he took his gloves and did a test wash. *Delicates*. Air dried. They came through looking fine, and if it reduced the life of the gloves—well, the gloves were expendable. He'd have to discard them after the Incident anyway. Only one more wash they'd have to endure, and that could wait until April.

From the garage he took a pair of pliers. He looked at the grooved tips. Perhaps they were as distinctive as a fingerprint, unique to this set of pliers. He got some duct tape and wrapped it around the pliers' grooves. Then he practiced picking up the gloves with the wrapped pliers, carrying around the gloves with the wrapped pliers, putting on the gloves with the wrapped pliers. This last part was a little difficult. He only had to use the pliers on one glove, of course, in order to keep his fingerprints off the gloves. Once one glove was in place, he could use it to pull on the other glove.

Just to be safe, one day after work he bought another pair of similar leather gloves. In case anyone asked, in some future time, what had happened to that pair of gloves, he could simply pass the new ones off as the old. Who would know?

And then the next night, a Friday night, he left the house after nine. He drove about an hour to a 24-hour Rite Aid he'd seen once in Ithaca. He looked around for a burner phone, but none were on display. Instead, he placed in his little blue basket a roll of high-quality packing tape, a spool of black thread, a stack of Post-it notes, a red bandana, several more cylinders of sterile wipes, a Sharpie, and—for the drive home—a can of iced coffee.

Colin wished he had facial hair or sunglasses; at least he had a sherpa hat on, pulled low over his ears. "Do you carry pre-paid phones here?" he asked the clerk.

"Yeah, they're back here somewhere," the clerk said. He pawed behind the counter through a shelf full of condoms and cigarettes. "Do you know what kind you want?"

"Disposable, with a pre-paid SIM card and a removable battery." Taking his own phone along on the day would be too dangerous, or course—he didn't even have it with him here, and this was an innocent trip to Ithaca—but Colin could imagine a number of situations that would call for a phone at hand, and he wouldn't want to be caught without one.

The clerk fumbled a plastic shell onto the counter. It looked adequate. "Thank you. Can you activate that for me?" A website accessed back in November had assured Colin the clerk could.

"Uggggggh," groaned the clerk, rolling his head and eyes. Perhaps it was the end of a long shift. But he did it. He had to unwrap the phone from the hard plastic, which required scissors and more groans, but he did it.

"Name," he asked.

"Brandon Wilson."

"Address?" and Colin did not give his real address. He paid cash.

45

The automatic door ushered Colin out of the store with his purchases. Once in the car he immediately removed the battery from the phone. He was wearing gloves, although he took them off when he started the car up, of course. The purchases were in a plastic bag. He wasn't crazy.

Once home, he tossed the empty iced coffee can, openly, into the recycling. It was not suspicious; anyone can drink iced coffee. He picked up a nail scissors in the bathroom and carried the plastic bag to the basement. There in the fluorescent light he put his gloves back on and took out the packing tape. It had an easy-start pull tab, which was lucky, because he could hardly pick at it with his nail while wearing gloves. He pulled off a piece and snipped it with the scissors, making sure to keep his gloved thumb on the roll so the loose end of the tape couldn't fall back against it. With the hand holding the tape he doubled the loose end over, making an ersatz tab. He put the long, dangling tape strand on the VHS tape holder, the one that had cracked. He taped right over the hardened slather of glue, wrapping the edge around. He practiced pulling several strips off, making sure he could do it easily with gloves. The test pieces he pulled off all went to reinforcing the VHS holder. Each time he made a little tab on the tape, for the next pull.

He put the tape roll back in the bag and carried it up two flights of stairs to his bedroom. He opened the drawer with the coveralls and went to upend the bag into it, when something brought him up short.

The top pair of coveralls were zipper-side up. He could have sworn he'd stored them zipper-side down. He'd certainly intended to—in the hopes that anyone glancing in the drawer would only see cloth. Was it possible that someone had been searching his house?

It sounded crazy, a crazy idea. He didn't want to be paranoid. He walked around, looking if anything else was out of place. The napkin with the address was still under the can of nuts. The rifle was just where he'd left it, of course.

Since his gloves were still on, he sat for a while in the basement, practicing switching clips. Then he got up and went out again, driving to another 24-hour

Rite Aid—this one much closer to home, over in Hesitania. He bought a door-knob, which was so thoroughly not suspicious that he almost considered using a credit card, for the points. He came home and installed the knob on the basement door with a screwdriver. It was the kind with a lock; it came with two keys, and he threaded one onto his keychain. The other one went into his junk drawer. By the time he was done it was well past one in the morning, so he went to bed.

There was still so much to do. Maybe tomorrow he could go to the library. Maybe he could drive around, scouting some locations. He still wanted to practice on his bike.

Then he remembered Carol. She'd be coming over.

9 Bernie smoked in the Pizza King parking lot. It was funny: He never craved a cigarette when he wasn't at work. He never smoked on his days off. ¶ Actually, this was one of his days off, but he'd had nothing to do, so he'd come back to the restaurant and joked around with the waitstaff until Mr. Prishtine had told him to get lost. Now he stood in the parking lot, mostly out of view, shivering in the night air, gazing through the window. It looked so warm and bright inside. One of the waitresses, Amber, was holding a pie on a silver tray up above her head, and she looked so impossibly beautiful when she laughed.

Maybe the people at the table were funny. He hoped they enjoyed their pizza.

10 The Sp!der sat in the basement, his mother's basement, drinking his think-ing drink: diet Coke with a packet of grape Kool-Aid powder mixed in. ¶ So John wanted to find out who this @CottinendKing was. Sp!der had said he'd get the dirt, of course, figuring it would be easy. @CottinendKing on Twitter was probably CottinendKing on some other network; find that email address on Facebook, say, and bingo! the job would be done.

But searching for CottinendKing brought up nothing. Emailcheckster.com said there was no email registered to CottinendKing at gmail, at hotmail, at aol. Sp!der brought up a tweet aggregator, loaded up every tweet CottinendKing had ever penned—there were only seventy-five of them—and searched in vain for the @ symbol, for the word email, even for the words dot and com. Finally he even read them all.

"Mickey! Your dinner's getting cold!"

"I'll be up soon, ma! Jeez!"

If Sp!der had been a real hacker, doubtless there would have been some back door he could have sashayed through. But Sp!der was a poser, and one dangerously close to being exposed, at least to John Oberman. He remembered the old techie motto: *hack the meatware*. It meant when you couldn't get in through computer tricks you could use human tricks. Figure out enough about someone and you'd know his password, which was inevitably a birthday or a kid's name.

But @CottinendKing was a cipher. There was nothing to latch onto. His bio on twitter just read "fuck all yall."

The only clues, then, were what he had tweeted about, and these tweets Sp!der pored over like a kabbalist, looking for any information. @CottinendKing liked wrestling, especially someone named Organ Grinder. He liked threatening violence. Said violence was going to go down in two months. He was not a skilled speller.

"Mickey! I'm not waiting any longer!"

All through his mother's famous spaghetti, Sp!der fumed. His mother clucked and fussed around him and that wasn't helping either.

He wanted to feel like he had left no stone unturned, but actually he had only turned over a couple of stones. It was like a labyrinth with only two or three short corridors, all dead ends. There wasn't even the satisfaction of getting lost in it!

Organ Grinder. Violence. Bad speller. Sp!der read the collection of tweets over again. "…body parts flin then whose sory…"

"This guy is an idiot," thought the Sp!der.

And some time the next night, around three in the morning, Sp!der had an idea. He made a new Twitter account, @WinFatBux4Life.

Would he have to lay down a series of false tweets to make his scam more plausible?

Nah, the guy was an idiot.

"@CottinendKing," Sp!der typed; "We are pleased to inform you that you have won…"

11 Carol had been afraid it might be awkward, seeing someone from work. They weren't in the same department, so it wasn't against any official rules, but maybe it would be—frowned upon?

But no one cared. In the morning Colin came by her desk on the third floor and kissed her hello, or brought her coffee. They didn't come in to work together—that might have been a little much. The one time he'd slept over on a weeknight—it had been raining so hard that night—they'd driven in in separate cars. Fortunately Colin had had a spare set of work clothes in his trunk; he said he always kept it there, for emergencies. He seemed like a man prepared for emergencies.

He wasn't secretive—Colin, she meant. He was open about everything except one thing, which appeared to be the *core thing*. When his mother called while Carol was over, he made introductions and passed her the phone. He made no secret of their relationship. He kissed her on the street, as well as at work. He was far from controlling. She wandered around his house freely; the only request he had made was that she not go in the basement, which, he said, was embarrassingly filthy. She tried the door once, and it was locked. Anyway, the rest of the house was pristine.

She'd known, in the past, her share of terrible boyfriends—not the cruel kind, but the kind who had no inner life, nothing but a few football teams and a brand of beer. Their idea of sex was indistinguishable from a TV show about sex. They talked about boobs but they never understood them. They barely even qualified as human, although they had a glib ability to ape the species, at least in the short term.

And Colin could look at first like he was waving a series of similar red flags. He didn't own a single book. He approached the more accessible arts—music, film—with an ironic detachment that made in unclear whether he actually enjoyed even the media he owned. When he spoke about himself it was probably to tell an amusing anecdote from his childhood—the teen summer he'd spilled gasoline on the lawnmower and then went to mow the lawn anyway, and the heat of the sun on the metal lawnmower casing hit the gasoline flashpoint and the whole machine erupted into flames etc.—that kind of thing.

But he lacked the terrible boyfriend's triviality. He clearly had great ambition, although he never revealed what the ambition was. He might have been an Emily Dickinson, his dresser drawers filled up with a secret poetic oeuvre; he might have been studying Fermat's Last Theorem; like some nineteenth century German Romantic genius, he was looking deeper into things—or something—than the rest of us rabble.

He reminded Carol of herself if she had not been such a failure.

12 Colin biked in the mornings, before work, with a removable light on the handlebars. It was bitter cold in early February. He started in the dark and by the time he got home the sun was coming up. He kept careful time with his wristwatch, so he would't be late. He wore an orange safety vest.

At first he was just making sure he could bike without losing his wind. He went at random, but favored small roads with less traffic. In his back pocket was the foldable map of Cottinend. He usually had his cell phone on him, but he didn't like looking at the map on it.

He went down plenty of dead end streets, but never Coronet. He kept his distance. But the unfolded map had shown him that Coronet ran parallel to Rano Boulevard, a cut-through street that of course did not dead end. The backyards of the houses on Rano abutted the backyards of the houses on Coronet. He rode a couple of times down Rano, trying to time it so the sun was already peeking out by the time he got there. He stopped to take a swig of water, perhaps more often than a biker would ordinarily. He was looking idly over between the houses on the north side of Rano. He was looking to see who had a fence.

One morning he found a discarded duffel bag on the side of the road, empty and ratty. He was wearing gloves already, so, after looking up and down the street to make sure no one was around, he scooped it up and hung it on the handlebars. An untraceable bag. Just some random street whose name he'd soon forget. He rode straight home and brought the bag to the basement. The boots fit inside just fine. He should probably get on the ball and do something about these boots! With a pair of needle-nosed pliers, the tips covered with duct tape, he carefully threaded the laces through the boots. By that time, he had to hurry through his shower and skip breakfast. He didn't want to be late for work, simply because he was never late for work, and any deviation from the routine would be suspicious.

"Hey, Colin," Carol said as he walked past her desk. He walked past her desk every day now, and kissed her on the cheek.

He put on a serious face. "Can I have a rain check on dinner tonight?" he asked. "My mother called and she says she's out of socks. You know she's going to make a federal production of it if I don't…"

"No, of course, go, go." She seemed worried, and Colin let himself get lost in the moment. She looked so charming with her fretful eyes and uplifted brow. He was doing all right. Then he went to work.

After work, Colin did indeed go sock shopping, but only for himself. Several pairs of thick, black socks, completely unremarkable. He drove home, and with his car in the garage and the lights out no one would know he was there. He was in the basement, and the basement had no windows.

The socks went through the washing machine, and then the drier, and then back in the wash, for a dozen cycles. After a while Colin wasn't sure why he was running them through the paces like this. It was nearly four in the morning. They were obviously already clean.

Colin put one pair of socks on, still warm from the drier. Then he put on his gloves and brought out the boots. He tried getting his feet into the boots, gloves still on, which proved surprisingly difficult. He went upstairs and rummaged through his sock drawer until he found an old shoehorn he'd stuck in the back.

After some practice he wiggled into the boots. He took them off. He considered getting a couple of hours sleep, but decided an early start was better. There was something he'd been meaning to do anyway.

He balled up the five extra pairs of socks and lined them up on top of the drier. He could put them in the drawer later. The boots went into the found duffel, along with a plastic bag from the grocery store. Colin changed into his biking clothes. He bundled up, of course. After a few minutes riding he'd warm up, but even then, the windchill could be brutal.

On his way out of the house, he stopped and looked up a number in the phone book, jotting it down on a Post-it. When he took the Post-it off the pad, he took not only the top sheet, but also the five or six sheets underneath it, leaving them all glued together. They went into his pocket, along with the shoehorn.

The duffel was slung over his shoulder as he wheeled his bike out of the garage. His phone was charging at home. Perhaps as an afterthought, he took the Post-its out of his pocket, rolled them up, and slid them into the hollow space at the end of his handlebars.

Ten minutes away, by bicycle, were a series of paved biking trails that wound through the woods. Hiking trails snaked all around them, sometimes running alongside, sometimes crossing. Technically the trails opened at sunrise, posted, but Colin doubted anyone really cared if he went there early. He biked to the trail, pulled his bicycle behind a tree and locked it to itself with the chain. He left the bike light on to see by. Sitting on a log, and without removing his gloves, he slid off his biking shoes and put them in the plastic bag. The plastic bag in the duffel. With the shoehorn he wrestled the new boots on.

Then he started walking. The bike light, detached from the handlebars and held like a flashlight, illuminated the trail faintly, but well enough to avoid tripping on a root. The boots were a little uncomfortable, as new boots will be. At least here among the trees the wind was less biting.

For two hours, thinking only of the plan, Colin walked back and forth along a small stretch of hiking trail. By the time he was unlocking his bicycle, his face was numb and his feet were killing him. All this to break in the boots, break them in without leaving prints around his lawn, without getting all over the soles any dirt or carpet fibers that might be recognized as his. Maybe it was too much, but he didn't know what was too much. And what else was he going to do?

The boots went back in the duffel bag, and the old biking shoes went on. For once he took off his orange safety vest and stuck it in his pocket. Colin started riding towards home, but turned aside. The orange vest flapped, half-out of his pocket. There was one lone payphone left in town, down by the Mobil station, and a day he was out with no cell phone was as good a day as any to stop by. The phone company would have a record of the call, of course, but no cell phone GPS would tie Colin to the area. He was straddling his bike as he stood in front of the payphone. He took off one glove to get a quarter from his pocket, but he put the glove back on, simply for the purpose of warmth. He fished the Post-its from the handlebar, just in case he misremembered, which he did not, the number and dialed. It rang eight times.

"Gaaaah?" said a voice.

"Bernard Feldstein?" said Colin. He found himself lowering his voice an octave, unintentionally; but having started at that pitch he thought it would be weird to stop, so he kept doing it. It made him sound, in his head, like a child playing at being the president.

"Who? Who calls me Bernard?" He had obviously just woken up.

Colin had kept himself absolutely clean for three months. He had made no attempt to contact his accomplice. There was nothing tying the two of them together except one brief meeting on one forgettable night in the back of a bar. Colin was not even sure he'd be able to pick the poor kid out of a lineup.

"I'm calling about April tenth."

"Omigod! Theodore Anderson!"

Colin almost said, "Who?" Then he remembered that Theodore Anderson—the name, slightly modified, of his junior high gym teacher—was what he'd passed himself off as. The problem with lying was that it was so hard to remember what you were improvising!

"This is Theodore Anderson," he said. "Have you told anyone about our scheduled meeting?"

"No! No, swear to God!"

"Good. Just to confirm your identity: Where do you work?"

"Oh! Pizza King. I do deliveries."

Colin ticked off an imaginary box in his head. He'd dimly remembered that Bernie had mentioned a job in a pizza parlor, and had long feared it was Choice Pizza. This was one worry gone.

"Good. Listen closely, there's something I need you to do. What day to do you have garbage pickup?"

"Friday night. I mean Saturday morning"

"On the evening of the tenth you have to take your garbage can and put it at the end of the driveway."

"Is the tenth a Friday?"

"No. I wouldn't have to tell you to do it if the tenth were a Friday. Take the can out anyway, and—this is important—make sure it's empty."

"You mean the toter?"

"Yes, the toter. Make sure it's empty."

"But what do I do with the garbage?" Bernie whined.

"Bernie, the whole reason we're trusting you is because of your resourcefulness. You can be resourceful, can't you?"

"Yes, of course! Trust me!"

"Good. Don't forget the toter. And of course you must be careful not to give anyone any hints about your mission."

"I won't!"

Colin wasn't sure how far he should push this. *A little further just to be sure,* he figured. "There might be spies everywhere. Don't let them even begin to get an idea that something is up." He really milked the presidential baritone.

Afterwards, he simply dropped the Post-its in the trash can at the gas station. Nothing suspicious about that. He happened to glance in the garbage can and saw three pieces of white cardboard, the kind that come in a new dress shirt. They weren't exactly what Colin had been looking for, but they were close enough. He'd wanted something black, but he could always color them in with the Sharpie he'd bought. Still a lucky find—untraceable. He glanced over his shoulder, fished the cardboard out, and stuck them in his duffel. He could do some arts and crafts after work. It was getting late.

At home he chugged three cups of coffee and took a shower. He had perhaps overdone it with the new boots; he put bandaids on the blisters. In work shoes he stepped into the car.

As he drove to work he rehearsed a humorous story about his mother and socks. It was important to keep that in mind about lies, that they were hard to remember if you made them up on the fly. A little rehearsal could keep the lie in your memory; a little rehearsal was all it took.

But then he decided a humorous story was all wrong. He decided to say he was worried about his mother.

Just to make sure, at lunch he called Sunset Grove and said he was worried about his mother.

13 Bernie hung up the phone. He was shaking. Here he was, standing in his underwear in the kitchen, by the old wall phone that never rang any more. He didn't even remember getting up to answer the phone; he must have come downstairs on sleepy autopilot. How did he answer the phone and what did he say? He hoped he hadn't sounded like an asshole.

But then he remembered, not what he said but what he'd heard. Quickly he grabbed a pen and jotted down, on the piece of paper on the fridge, "garbge out" [sic].

There was light coming through the side windows, so it clearly was not the middle of the night. All the clocks in the downstairs were just 12:00 blinking, so he headed back to his bedroom to see on his cell phone how many hours of sleep he had left. *A lot.*

He crawled into bed, but with the phone in his hand he automatically checked Twitter. He followed several hundred people he had never met in real life; everyone he knew in real life thought Twitter was (in Stone's words) "for homos." But today there was something so unusual he almost overlooked it. A notification, and when he tapped through…

"We are pleased to inform you…"

"Holy shit!" said Bernie to himself. "Anderson knows everything!"

14 Yes, yes, Colin finally got to the library and looked up what streets had Wednesday-morning garbage pickup. He used his phone for other searches, of course. Under the circumstances it wasn't even suspicious to begin googling *adult onset dementia.* In fact, it was better to keep a record of these searches! The phone was perfect for this, but at times he sneaked a quick search in at work, just to leave another trail.

He cleared some extra space in his garage so that he could drive his car three or four feet forward without fear of hitting a lawn mower. He bought some exfoliant and an electric razor—these he could buy just anywhere. He'd never used an electric razor before. He plugged it into a basement outlet to charge. The next day, in the bathroom, he carefully shaved the backs of his hands, from his knuckles to the tops of his wrists. He tried to "fade" the cut gradually into his arm hair. He was fair enough that a casual glance should spot no difference. He cleaned up the hairs and moved the razor back to the basement.

With his eyes closed he practiced closing and opening the combination lock on his bicycle. It had three dials, each 0 to 9, and if he moved one dial one click one way when he locked it, he could move it a click the other way to unlock it without even looking.

There was a three-foot chainlink fence behind his yard, separating him from a neighbor he'd never met. When he returned from his morning bike-and-hike he went in the back and practiced vaulting over it: one hand on top, and, with a glove on, the tops of the chains sticking up didn't dig into his hand as he'd feared they would. It was easy and it didn't hurt. Just in case, he kept practicing, several mornings, back and forth, after a bike-and-hike, before he went in for a shower.

He brought his burner phone along on one early morning bike ride and tested it. The battery was mostly full. The phone had actual physical press buttons that he could use with gloves on, so Colin dialed the time and an infomercial's 800 number, trying not to let the phone touch his ear or the condensation of his breath; and it seemed to work fine, as a phone. He probably wouldn't even need it.

And one day Colin told Carol he was interested in finding the best slice of pizza in Cottinend. A project! She seemed surprised, but was willing on weekends to get takeout slices for lunch, a different place each time. Sometimes they both went and sometimes it was just Colin and sometimes it was just Carol, bringing a little square box back while the other one set the table—a trivial task for pizza. When Carol was going alone, Colin suggested Pizza King, just to get it out of the way. When Colin went alone—it was on a terrifying day, a stupid blunder he didn't even want to think about—he went to Choice, pulling deliberately into a corner of the rear parking lot, where a dumpster stood. He put on sunglasses and an old checkered cap he had that he hadn't worn for years. He took a moment to walk around the car, feigning he was looking for dents; but his eye, behind the shades, was trained on the back of the dumpster. He was confirming there was a sturdy handle there. He took a moment to drop a small scrap of paper, wadded up and drawn from his pocket, into the dumpster's maw. Then he got the slices quickly, and left. He was proud of having established a pattern of going to pizza parlors, but he didn't like the fact that he had stopped in himself. It seemed sloppy, and the hat and shades were no proper disguise, really. Too much today had been sloppy.

He brought the pizza back to Carol's place and broached the subject of his mother.

"I know you said you were worried about her..." Carol began, trailing off invitingly.

"It's just the senior moments; they're getting more common, you know? She'll tell me a story and then three minutes later she'll tell me the same story."

"I haven't noticed; on the phone, I mean," Carol said.

"It's not always like that," Colin agreed. "But I'm afraid it's more likely to get worse than get better. I was thinking it might be time for her to move—"

"For her to move in with you?" Carol said, surprised.

"Oh, good grief no! No, I just meant she should move closer. Do you know Ridgemont Rest?"

"No?"

"It's a senior facility. It's not a home, it's just assisted living. I mean, it's more or less like the place she's at now, except it's right here in Cottinend, just north of the highway."

Carol nodded, but she seemed unsure of what to say.

"I mean—I don't know what it's like. I've never been there, obviously. I've just driven past. I drove past today. I mean—would you go see it with me?"

"See it?"

"I just want to look at the place. See the facilities and everything. It gets good reviews, but I'd want to see it. Just so I know in case it becomes, you know, necessary."

"Yes, of course I'd go with you."

"Thank you. I hate this pizza, by the way."

"Really," Carol said. "I thought it was pretty good."

"This one and Pizza King, they really kind of made me feel sick. I'd prefer," he said this part carefully, "to avoid them in the future."

15 As Carol settled into the transition from assemblage-of-dates to in-a-relationship—not that they talked about being in a relationship—she never stopped worrying at the strange secret genius of Colin Lang.

He had a quirky, almost childlike charm. After a month and a half of dating, she was holding his hand as they watched an old movie and she realized—

"Why is your wrist so smooth?" she asked.

"Oh! The arm hairs were catching in my watchband, so I shaved my left wrist. Then to balance it out I shaved my right."

She ran her hands over his.

"My mother hasn't even noticed," he said.

Nevertheless: She had promised herself, long ago, that she'd be fussier about relationships. It was too easy to find a guy in perpetual adolescence who sleepwalked through life without tastes, without opinions, without long-term bonds, without ambitions that did not involve video games or the consumption of pornography. Maybe she'd been too fussy about relationships, so long had she been without one—but she had *also* promised herself that once in a relationship she would not obsess over a guy, whatever his admirable, curious, or fascinating qualities. She was Carol Wernick and she would never be one of those women who was a cipher, her tastes and opinions a collection of the tastes and opinions of old boyfriends.

Was she following through on her promises? Was she perhaps spending too much time picking at the knotty clue of Colin Lang? And Colin himself—were his apparent red flags perhaps actual red flags?

There was one time, for example. He'd terrified her. She was standing in his kitchen sipping coffee in a robe. He had just dressed, preparing to go out for a slice of pizza. It was almost noon, but they always lingered in bed on a Saturday, only rising to sit on the glassed-in patio and watch the birds come to the feeder Carol had bought him. Sometimes Colin would fry up some eggs, but often enough lunch was the first meal of the day. That's the way it was today, and Carol was getting hungry.

"Mind if I grab a snack while you're out?" she asked.

"Help yourself," Colin called back. He was putting his shoes on over by the side door, the one that faced the garage.

Carol opened the pantry and leaned in. She couldn't see Colin with her head in the pantry—from the chair he was sitting in, he could probably only see her butt sticking out—but she kept up a polite little chatter as she poked around. "Crackers...rice cakes...oh! Maybe I'll have a few mixed nuts." Along those lines.

The way he shouted then...she'd never heard such a strange voice, certainly not from Colin and probably not anywhere outside of a movie. "Stop!" he shouted, but *shouted* does not do it justice, his terrified, terrifying voice. She froze. She was genuinely scared; for a moment she thought he was going to kill her, and of course standing stock still was not the smartest thing to do when someone was going to kill you. She wasn't proud of that.

He didn't kill her, of course, and he didn't so much push her as slide himself between her and the pantry shelves. She saw him scoop the mixed nuts up into a hug—there was no other way to describe it. Clutching it to his chest, his fists balled up, he slid back out of the pantry. He turned his back for a moment, then turned around and stood there looking at her. One hand held the can of nuts; the other was casually in his pocket.

"Sorry," he said, "I was afraid it was a snake."

Carol just stood there, breathing fast.

"I didn't want it to scare you," he added.

"A...snake?" Carol managed.

"I mean the mixed nuts. A fake can with a spring snake inside. I used to have one. I didn't want it to scare you."

"*You* scared me."

"Yeah, I didn't think it through. I was reacting on instinct. I didn't want the snake to spring out, you jump, your coffee goes flying..."

"I'm not holding my coffee."

"Yeah, well, I see that now."

He really did look contrite. Or he looked something. He looked ashamed, at least.

Then he went and got pizza and everything was all right. In fact, he asked her —it was such an intimate request for people who had only been dating a couple of months—to go look at old folks' homes with him, for his mother. It touched her heart, and of course she was happy to go. He called one immediately and set up an appointment for the next day. Carol would have put it off for a week, or more, and perhaps she had not anticipated having to go see the place so quickly. Perhaps she had not anticipated an official tour.

Because the tour was deadly boring. Carol wasn't sure, but she could swear Colin paid more attention to the parking lot than the actual facilities. And his questions were weird. He kept asking about security.

"To prevent elopement?" asked the tour guide, an oleaginous older woman who reminded Carol of her middle-school principal. Actually, everything about the facility reminded her of middle school.

"Yes," said Colin, "to prevent elopement."

The guide went through a serious of lockdowns and checkpoints that all sounded to Carol like a fire hazard. But she wasn't really paying attention.

"And if the tenant elopes? Are there security guards patrolling that would see her leaving?"

"Our attendants are very vigilant, and are more than sufficient to apprehend any elopers."

Colin ended the tour soon after that. Carol asked him, in the car, what he thought.

"It was generally untidy," he said, something she hadn't noticed. "And if they're lax janitorially, how can I trust them in anything else?"

"At least they're close to your new favorite pizza place," she tried saying with a big smile.

"Choice Pizza! Barf!" he said with a laugh, and at a red light he kissed her.

16 Sp!der's phone rang and he knew it was John Oberman before he even looked. ¶ "I'm working on it," he said as he picked up. ¶ "Working on it? Sp!der, it's already the end of February."

"Now, February is a very short mo—"

"I need to find this guy."

"John, John. I have several irons in the fire. They should pay off before April."

"Irons? What does that mean?"

"You know, you're not paying me, John."

Oberman was yelling. "You didn't try to contact him, did you?"

"Give me some credit," Sp!der said.

"Did you see what he posted today? Four or five hundred dead?"

"Wait what?" Sp!der tucked the phone up against his shoulder and reached for his keyboard. He hadn't gotten a response to his last gambit, and it had been two weeks, but he'd just assumed the target had not logged into Twitter. Yet there it was: "400 or 500 dead coming soon not in a theter its all 2 real son!!!" [sic].

After a flurry of soft soap, Sp!der uncharacteristically hurried Oberman off the phone. He sat in his swivel chair and thought. Perhaps the King of Cottinend was smarter than he typed.

"This looks like a job for Ilyana," thought Sp!der.

Ilyana *was* Sp!der, of course—one of his troupe of players; an identity he kept plausibly active on the internet so she could chime in and agree with or praise Sp!der should he need backup. Whenever Sp!der felt challenged, all the players could come out: Cowboy Rex and Big Steve, but mostly the ladies: Sue McCormick and Gertie and Pepper Anne and seven different attractive foreign women with pictures lifted from websites devoted to Russian brides. Natasha and Anastasia and all their friends each had a Facebook page and a Twitter account and more than one dating profile, with which they each kept several gentlemen strung along. Ilyana had been liking and sharing things for years. She looked legitimate.

She was going to have to develop a crush on @CottinendKing.

17 As soon as Carol noticed that he'd been shaving his hands, Colin stopped hiding the electric razor in the basement. Now it had become normal and normal was not suspicious.

It was good to have a rule of thumb like that.

18 No, Colin wasn't secretive, Carol thought. If anyone was secretive, that would be Carol. ¶ Her parents lived a half-hour drive away, and she hadn't brought Colin over for dinner yet. Her parents were both academics, and humanities academics to boot. They had never understood Carol's obsession with numbers—her father had in fact taken her aside in her adolescence and tried to persuade her that the concept of quantification was…colonialist or patriarchal or something bad. They would never understand Colin, and the whole dinner would be filled with casual references to Adorno or Habermas, people that Colin would assume were relatives.

Colin simply didn't have the artsy background. She'd gone with him to a museum in Albany for an exhibition of antique Gustave Doré prints, and he'd had only the most cursory knowledge of what they were illustrating: not just the obscure ones—L'Épine's *Croquemitaine* or whatnot—but *Don Quixote*, "The Raven," the *Divina Commedia*.

But he was interested, and he studied the old sheets with an attentive eye. Several of the images from Dante's *Inferno* he lingered over so long Carol began to get restless.

Finally he seemed to snap out of it. He looked sheepish. "Why aren't they yellowing?" he asked the docent, who explained about acidity levels in paper. Colin thanked him.

On the drive home he said, "Never had a girl ask me to see her etchings before."

"They seemed to speak to you," Carol said.

"Now that was some good art," Colin agreed, and if she brought him to her parents' they would write Doré off as mere illustration. One of her mother's most prized possessions was one half of an Adolph Gottlieb painting—an original, but it had somehow been damaged, and only the top part remained, depicting a maroon circle and nothing else.

How do you even tell your parents, past thirty, "Mom, dad, I met a new fella"? They had certainly noticed she hadn't been visiting.

"Busy at work?" her mother asked archly.

"Mom, did you see what the president said?"—and that would distract her.

Of course Carol was embarrassed by her parents; but she was also afraid: What if they didn't see in Colin Lang the ineffable thing she could not articulate?

The ineffable depth?

19 Oberman hadn't know who Cassandra was until the Chief started calling him that. *Cassandra, Cassandra.* At first he assumed it was just a random girl's name. *Ha ha, Oberman's a girl, a girl named Cassandra.* But finally he looked it up and learned that Cassandra was a prophet that no one ever listened to.

"Cassandra was right, you know," Oberman told the Chief.

"Yeah, well, you're not," said the Chief. And that should have been that. But Oberman had a feeling about these Twitter threats.

"We don't even know he lives near here," Campbell objected for the hundredth time. "He hasn't said what he's going to do or where. He could be playing a video game. After all, he *is* on Twitter."

"Twitter is not a video game," Oberman pointed out, also for the hundredth time.

Campbell took Oberman's phone out of his hand and looked at the latest outburst. *Four or five hundred dead.* "Tell you what," Campbell said. "He makes one more good scary threat like that and I'll send it up the chain of command."

But no more tweets came. Not one more threat. In fact, the whole account disappeared, and with it Oberman's one chance to be right.

20 It happened like this. It was because of Randall Adler. ¶ Randall Adler had moved to Brooklyn for a year and had returned to Cottinend an ironic boxer. He had a handlebar mustache and a tattoo of John L. Sullivan (1858–1918), and he boxed with his bare knuckles, the fist held palm-down. He came over with weed, and Stone came over with beer, and Bernie greeted them at the door and pretended to be pleased to see Randall. The man who always had ideas. That was his brand, and he put it on his business cards: *Randall Adler, the man who always has ideas.*

Today he had an idea for revenge. "The thing to do is," he said as he rolled a joint, "is to make sure your enemy, when he dies, gets buried in a really crowded place, like Times Square."

"Why's that? Why's that?" Stone asked, for Stone was forever eager.

Randall was really taking his time with that joint, packing it precisely, but *theatrically* precisely. "If someone walks on your grave—your future grave, I mean—you get a chill down your spine, right? Everyone knows that. So if your grave is going to be someplace mad busy, people be walking over it all the time. You get nonstop chills."

"What would I want nonstop chills?" Bernie broke in, annoyed. He was annoyed by the fake urban patois Randall inconsistently affected. He was annoyed by how slow Randall was, and how cheap-ass the beer Stone brought.

Randall paused for effect. "You don't want chills. You want your enemy to have chills. That's the revenge. He'll go crazy! Literally out of his head. The endless treading on his grave will drive him to an early death, and that—" here he waved the completed but unlit joint "—is fortunate because otherwise you wouldn't have the opportunity to bury him where you wanted. Just make sure it's someplace busy or the whole plan won't work!"

Bernie had a hard time making heads or tails of this while tipsy, and it only got worse after he was thoroughly wasted. He had half a mind to put Randall in his place, let him know who around here was being contracted for a vigilante squad of some sort (the details were fuzzy); but he remembered the WinFatBux contest account on Twitter. Spies were everywhere. He rarely tweeted at all any-more, although he did check obsessively for other spies and their traps. He set-tled on the simple riposte: "Oh yeah?"

"Yeah," said Randall.

What happened next made sense at the time, although to a sober mind, such as, even, the minds of the three participants the next day, it all seemed a random jumble of unrelated events. Randall decided to challenge his pals to a boxing match. Bernie remembered what his father'd used to say, to wit, "Always wrestle a boxer," so he tackled Randall. They wrestled for a while—it was more like Bernie getting his ass kicked all over the room—and then Stone jumped on both of them and they all three wrestled until they bumped into the television and knocked it off the stand. Then they spent a lot of time making sure it wasn't bro-ken, which was hard to do because they kept dropping it when the tried to pick it up, and the batteries fell out of the remote and rolled beneath a chair so they had trouble turning it on. Miraculously it still worked. It was apparent that Stone had been the best wrestler, but Randall explained that the poor amateur had made a lot of technical errors, and anyone who really knew a lot about wrestling would see that in a heartbeat. Bernie, who assumed he knew more about wrestling than either of these other shitheads, agreed reflexively.

They ran out of weed, but Bernie had some whipped cream in the fridge, so they probably did whippets. Certainly they did *something* else. A lot of the night was fuzzy. Sometime in the middle of things Randall proposed leaving the house to get more beer. There he is fumbling with the deadbolt (it was unlocked).

Bernie was thinking. He had a tattoo he'd gotten last summer: It was a smiley face with squinting eyes over the words CHARLIE DON'T SURF. Bernie couldn't remember what it was a reference to, but he thought it was a reference to some-thing. He also thought it might be racist, so he couldn't exactly go around asking just anyone what it meant. He couldn't ask Stone because Stone would make fun of him for not remembering. Stone had been there when he'd got it. But (Bernie reasoned) if Stone went to get beer instead of Randall, certainly he could ask

Randall about the tattoo, even though when soberer he would avoid being alone with the irritating man.

But as much as Bernie pushed for Stone to go get the beer, it was Randall, loudly insisting he was in a better condition to drive, who left. Just then Bernie and Stone realized they actually had plenty of beer in the fridge, and when they ran outside to catch him before he reached his car, they found Randall lying in the lawn, face down. They dragged him back in to the house and slapped him until he vomited on the kitchen floor. Then he got up and demanded a singing contest. Only at that point did Bernie realize Randall had left his pants on the lawn.

"You don't need pants to do the victory dance," Randall sang.

The singing contest went ahead, marred only by Randall's ironic love of bad music: boy bands, jazz, and TV themes. Finally things ground to a halt over a disagreement about how many na na nas were in one particular My Chemical Romance song. Randall vowed to prove he was right, but of course his phone was somewhere on the lawn. Stone's and Bernie's phones were also missing, fallen out, no doubt, during the wrestling match. They shuffled around the living room, the three of them, on hands and knees, while Stone made mooing noises. Just as Randall announced that he was going to be a cowboy, Stone came up with Bernie's phone, covered in dust bunnies from deep beneath the couch.

He swiped it on. The first thing he must have seen—so often this would be the case—would have been the Twitter app, and the part of the Twitter app Bernie had left it on was his notifications There was a new notification, from a certain @barista_Ilyana, who had tagged Bernie with some extremely salacious requests, accompanied by a comparatively chaste photograph of a blonde woman in a one-piece bathing suit.

"Bro!" Stone sang out. "This tight Russian hottie is begging for a smash."

Bernie was up in a shot, goggling over Stone's shoulder. But Randall grabbed him and moved him aside. As Bernie struggled to see what they were talking about, Randall read, "'Barista Ilyana.' Oh, she wants your venti."

"Let me see," Bernie said.

67

"This is not a drill. Repeat, this is not a drill," said Stone.

Randall started stammering out something—apparently a joke about how he'd like to drill this barista—but he must have been too drunk, stoned, and tired; it came out unfunny and slightly incoherent. But in his moment of concentration on wordplay, he let down his guard enough to give Bernie a peek over the shoulder at the phone. Bernie began to scream.

"Give me that! Give me that!"

"Jesus, dude! Chill!"

"Give me that! Give me that!" Bernie punched Stone in the ear, and Stone dropped the phone. Bernie pounced on it. Spies were everywhere! The Russians were in on it! He scuttled on his knees and one hand to the bathroom, into which he locked himself. He could hear the other two laughing outside. He checked the phone. Indeed, the crude come-on was, he thought, transparently false; women like this did not come on to Bernie Feldstein; but he could dimly perceive that in another situation, on another night, he might have fallen for it. In a panic he deleted his Twitter account. Pressing CONFIRM felt like pulling the trigger, the pistol between his eyes. He was breathing heavily.

When he opened the door, he saw that Stone did not appear to be hurt. Bernie was somewhat relieved, but also disappointed and embarrassed. He'd really slugged the boy! Stone should be down for the count.

"What the hell was that about?" Stone said.

"That's my phone," Bernie whined, after a brief pause in which he failed to think up a lie.

"You got nudes?" Randall said.

"No."

"Show me your dick so I know you're not gay," Randall said.

"No."

And after a few extra minutes of awkwardness, they were the same, again, as they had been. Not necessarily people who liked each other, all of them, but nevertheless people who were still pretty blitzed.

"We have to have a dance contest," Randall said.

But they didn't have a dance contest. They ended the night, which is to say greeted the morning, lying on the floor listening to Randall explain that the death of any one individual had no meaning, because everyone an individual had touched or affected, a whole community, would live on.

"But what if that community died, too?" Stone wanted to know.

Well, opined Randall, that wouldn't matter either, because the "nation state" (his term) would endure.

"But what if the whole country dies?" Stone asked.

Still no problem. Humanity would endure.

"And if everyone, all people, die?"

We have come to understand that all of history is just leading to the rise of mammals. Whales and tigers and the top of the food chain. Mammals would still endure.

"Sure, but what if mammals all become extinct?"

Okay, but life would still be there. The planet would still be teeming with life.

"But what if the Earth falls in into the sun? Kaboom and that's it?"

It was no big deal. There was still the universe, wasn't there? And what were you going to do about that?

"'I don't care if I die because there are rocks in space.' Is that really your argument?"

But Bernie was lying with his feet on his mom's old chair and his head in a pile of crumbs—*had they eaten something?—how old were these crumbs?*—thinking about the barista. "I want 2 gargle yr american balls" [sic]. He wasn't going to fall for something like that.

He could feel himself getting smarter.

21 Agatha Law, resident of Nassau County, was visiting her parents in Hobsons Falls, so Carol met up with her on a Sunday for old time's sake. It had been over ten years since they'd seen each other in person, although of

course the firehose of social media had made Carol already bored of Aggie's career, her marriage, her adorable children, and her catchphrase: "There is only one law: Agatha Law!"

Nevertheless, Aggie didn't want to talk about herself at all. Carol immediately felt guilty. She hadn't even bothered to go look up the kids' names, assuming they would have been thrown at her in minute one.

Instead, Aggie said: "Bitch, you have to tell me about this man of yours!"

Somehow, this was much worse than the career and the children. "I don't know what to say," Carol said.

"Come on, dish! What's he like? What's he do? How's he...?" She somehow managed to convey, with the trailing off and the eyebrows, something far more vulgar and lascivious than if she'd just come out and asked about their sex life.

"Shouldn't we talk about something else?" Carol asked. Added to her previous embarrassment was this, now: the implication that the last ten years of her life, her career and her loneliness and her desperate gambit in switching jobs were somehow less important than some two-month relationship.

But Aggie misinterpreted the reticence, and made a face that said: "Trouble in paradise?" So Carol had to jump in and speak before Aggie actually said: "Trouble in paradise?" which would have been unbearable.

She outlined, briefly, Colin's career aptitude, his solicitousness for mother, his easygoing kindness. You couldn't call him thoughtful, in the sense that he anticipated her needs, but he was always thinking. She tried, not very successfully, to explain his mysterious charisma, his unplumbable inner depth.

Aggie would have none of it, "Bitch, he's having an affair."

"I don't think he can have an affair, technically. I mean, we're just dating. We never even talked about...I mean, can you go steady over thirty? Is that a thing?"

"I mean that he has someone on the side."

"Would he have time?" Carol asked.

"What, are you together every day?"

"Well, yes, at work. But we have dinner many days."

"And you stay over?"

"No so much weeknights…"

"Uh huh," said Aggie. She was wearing large round sunglasses, which was a ridiculous choice in the overcast perpetual gloom of the New York–Pennsylvania corridor, but at least she had them pushed up and riding on her forehead.

"He gets up early and goes biking."

"'Biking'? In March? Right," said Aggie. "And where is he now?"

"He's visiting his mother. She's in a home in Salton."

"Sure he is. Have you met this 'mother'?" Before Carol could answer, Aggie went on:

"I've seen these 'deep' ones before. If he's not cheating on you, then he's gay. Oh, and then he's also definitely cheating on you."

"You've got him all wrong," said Carol, and she meant it.

But the next morning she woke up early and couldn't fall aback asleep. She decided to go pick up a bagel for breakfast and then, on a whim, she drove past Colin's house, and then several times in circles around the environs of Colin's house, until, as dawn cracked, she spotted him in a thick coat puffing along on a bicycle, a duffel bag swinging from his handlebars.

So he was bicycling—confirmed—but now Carol started to wonder if he was simply bicycling back from *somewhere*. From *someone's*.

At work, when he came by for a kiss, she mentioned tentatively that she remembered him saying he biked in the morning, and she wondered if she could join him one morning.

"Oh. Sure. Of course."

If he seemed surprised, he didn't seem panicky.

"How about tomorrow morning?" she asked.

"Sounds great. You'll have to bundle up. Want to pick up your bike after work and crash?"

"Crash?"

"Ha ha! That's not what I meant! Crash as in spend the night."

He was pleasant and natural about it. She had no idea, it turned out, how to get her bicycle in her car, so he came to her place. The bike trails he frequented, he said, which wound through the forested no man's land to the north, were nearer her house anyway.

In the morning they went for a bike ride so cold she regretted every moment. It felt like her face was cracking in half. Everything was uphill. Was this the kind of person she'd become? Suspicious and jealous of phantoms?

And yet there in the back of her mind was the horrible thought. The one thing Colin had not brought along on this bike ride, the only actual suspicious thing, was that ratty old duffel she'd seen on his handlebars the previous morning. His overnight bag? A toothbrush and a change of clothes, just right for transporting by bicycle?

It was also so dark here under the trees, and even though Colin had lent her his bike light it was still weird to ride with so little visibility. She was in the worst mood but had to keep smiling, for terrible reasons she could neither admit not understand.

The pavement was narrow enough that they mostly rode single file, with Carol in front to set pace. But when she stopped for a breather he'd pull up beside her. At one rest, as they straddled their bikes, Colin pointed at a hiking trail that crossed the bike path.

"Sometimes I bike up here and just lock up against a tree and go hiking," he said. "I bet it will be beautiful in the spring."

"You hike here?" Carol asked, too tired to flesh out the question properly.

"Yeah. Not every time but pretty often."

"Do you," she husbanded her scarce breath for this one, "what? Just hike in your sneakers?"

"No, no. I bring hiking boots with me."

"Hiking boots?"

"Sure. You, know I tote them along in a duffel bag. Then I just change right here on the trail. Are you all right?"

With relief and humiliation, and also increasingly with pain as ice-cold tears coursed down her bitter, freezing cheeks, Carol began to cry.

"I'm so sorry," she said. "Oh, Colin, I'm so sorry."

"Don't worry about it," he said with his hand on her upper arm—they could get no closer, could scarcely embrace on two bicycles. "Look, let's ride back to your place. It'll be all downhill from here."

Time destroy'd
Is suicide, where more than blood is spilt.
•Young, *Night Thoughts* (1742).

III. THE CRUELEST MONTH.

Colin Lang • Carol Wernick • John Oberman • Colin Lang • Stone & Randall •
Carol Wernick • Hunter Arnoux • Carol Wernick • The Sp!der • Colin Lang •
Carol Wernick • Bernie Feldstein • John Oberman • Colin Lang • Amber Meir •
John Oberman • The Sp!der • Carol Wernick • Colin Lang

1 He was impatient to make an early ask, just so that there were no delays, but he realized he'd have to wait another day, so it didn't look like an April fool. On April second, Colin went to his boss and had a serious talk. Colin's mother, who lived in Sunset Grove in Salton, was having problems with memory and with executive functioning. He was getting increasingly worried about her, and had even started weighing options about moving her closer—either to his own house, short-term, or to Ridgemont Rest right here in Cottinend.

But his mother was well established in Salton, and he was hesitant to remove her from both her care facility and her social support network, if they were actually good enough. And there was the delicate matter of breaking all of this to a mother who was having trouble remembering that there was even an issue here.

Therefore (Colin went on), as he had a significant amount of vacation time saved up, he would like to take a week or so off to spend the days at Sunset Grove; see on weekdays what he usually only saw on weekends; evaluate at greater length and in greater detail his mother's decline.

"You've really been 'cooking with gas' recently," Mr. Arnoux said with a sage nod. "Giving 110%. The least we can do is a little time off for personal matters."

"Thank you," said Colin.

"You want to decamp right away, I assume," Arnoux said more than asked.

"Oh, no," Colin said very quickly. "I have a few things I'd like to finish up here. I'd also have to contact Sunset Grove and make sure I can do what I'm looking to do. I don't actually know their regulations yet." Colin gave a few more reasons he had saved up, and the more he talked the more Arnoux's eyes narrowed.

"Colin," said Hunter Arnoux after a cautious pause, "you remember last November when you grew a beard for charity." Once again it was not a question, the way he said it.

"Yes," Colin nevertheless said.

"What did you do with the money you raised?" And that was a question.

Colin was aware he had said something wrong, or more precisely had said something in the wrong way. This should have been no surprise. He had never been an actor. It's possible that he had made an error in allowing himself two anomalous activities—the Movember and the vacation days—in one six-month span. Or perhaps he had just been, as liars often are, too *prepared*.

This made no sense—Colin was always prepared. Sometimes he made a foolish error, such as leaving Feldstein's address under those mixed nuts—completely unnecessary in retrospect, as the address was in the phone book—but it was hardly a question of not being prepared.

The only thing to do—and this was Colin's instinct; there was no time to think it out right now—was establish a pattern. Show that he was always prepared. And at least this was a question with an easy answer.

"All donations were made directly to the Movember Foundation, so I didn't see any of the money. I'm not sure if you participated, but you'd simply go to the website and search for my name. I was registered. Now, I did make a sizable donation myself, and of course I kept a record for tax purposes, but I'd have to check if the site keeps records of who else made a donation on that campaign."

"No, no, never mind. Idle curiosity. I was just..."—Arnoux fumbled around—"...'thinking outside the box.' Now what day were you planning on starting this?" Whatever suspicion had been there evaporated in embarrassment. Colin had played it right.

When to start? Assuming all went well when he called Sunset Grove: Friday, April sixth. He'd take eight work days off and be back at work on the sixteenth.

2 Samburn came in to the pizza place while Bernie was loitering between deliveries. Bernie thought this was a perfect chance to ask someone who wasn't Randall about his tattoo. Bernie had meant to look up Samburn come April, after his mission, when Bernard Feldstein was to have become famous. For Samburn had his own notoriety: Two years before he had almost robbed a bank. He'd had the brilliant idea to create a disguise by rubbing his face with poison ivy the day before the robbery; unfortunately, the reaction was worse than he'd expected, and his eyes swelled shut, and he'd never gotten to the bank. It was't even, technically, an attempted robbery; but he still had his bragging rights, for getting closer to such a crime than anyone else in town; and Bernie couldn't wait to hold his own head high. Higher than Samburn.

The head held high was a full week away, though. For the moment all Samburn was there for was to get quizzed about a tattoo.

"Actually, I want a slice," said Samburn. But Bernie said,

"Have you seen this?" and pulled up his shirt. The tattoo was on his shoulder blade. "Get it?" he asked.

"Yeah," said Samburn. "It's a little racist, though, isn't it?"

Before Bernie could ask for more detail, Amber served Samburn his slice; and then after he left of course she wanted to see Bernie's tattoo, too. Somewhat reluctantly, Bernie lifted the shirt over his protruding ribs and showed off his boney shoulder blade. "I don't get it," she said.

"I guess you'll have to google it," Bernie said. And then he could have kicked himself! Of course he could just google it! He started to laugh, just from relief, and that got Amber laughing too.

"You know," she said, "a bunch of us are going out to the Munster after work today. You should come along."

Bernie stopped laughing. *He was getting smarter.* "N–no," he stammered, remembering Ilyana. "I've got some…thing to do." There was only one explanation for a girl like Amber Meir wanting to sleep with him. He was too smart for that.

"Oh. Okay," said Amber. She was looking at him strangely. Did she know he knew?

About her?

If he couldn't trust Amber Meir, whom could he trust? Spies were everywhere and he was going to have to play this super smart and super cool.

"You can't be too careful nowadays," as his father always used to say.

3 Oberman should have let it drop, but he was not someone to let it drop. ¶ When the tweets dried up, whatever small interest he'd managed to coax out of the department dried up as well. The whole thing had been "exposed as a hoax," they claimed, when it had been exposed as no such thing.

Sp!der wasn't answering his phone which meant either that he was grounded or he had failed—the same result, really, those two.

"Don't you dare grandstand," Tabitha said.

Maybe, as the time since the last tweet grew longer, the grave reality of the situation should have lessened.But that's not how Oberman saw it. To Oberman, the time until April 10 was growing shorter every day.

4 Colin arranged everything with Sunset Grove. He finished up some projects and passed their dangling remainders along to team members. He would not be going to work during the day, and so there would be a different pattern than the rest of the year, but it would still be a pattern. He had to establish a pattern, of course.

On Friday he rose early, as though it were a work day, and got a quick bike ride and hike in. He felt invigorated. If nothing else, he was in better shape than he had been in years.

He fried some eggs for breakfast. Perhaps, he thought, he should listen to the radio while he ate. He had a dim memory of his father frying eggs while singing along to classic rock. But the only radio he owned was in his car. He considered getting up and putting a CD on, but then he figured he was better off focusing on the plan.

At nine, timed precisely, he was in the car, backing out of the driveway. He took Blande Boulevard to I-81. He was watching the traffic patterns, naturally. This would be the first time in years, holidays excepted, that he drove to Salton on a weekday. The Friday traffic was light. It was a nice day for April: clouds, but no rain.

He stopped at a rest stop off the highway to use the bathroom. He didn't want to be early. But perhaps even the precedent of the rest stop would come in handy.

The whole key was that he must act in a perfectly predictable way, every day, including the day of the Incident. As long as he kept to a pattern, there would be no reason to suspect him.

There was only one place that he allowed variation, and that was in his thoughts. All his life, his thoughts had been free when his body had ticked its clockwork way forward through time. Now, he explored different possibilities for the upcoming week. Especially, as he drove, he wondered what he would do with the spoiler, the one factor that had not been incorporated into the plan when he'd sketched it out last fall. What would he do about Carol?

5 In The Swan with Two Throttles, a dive bar on Flax Street, Stone and Randall sat drinking. They had decided to drink one each of every kind of drink they could think of until they passed out. They'd already had a beer, a margarita, a gin and tonic, and a Harvey Wallbanger each, and in pretty quick succession. It was Randall's turn to think of one, and he was already drunk.

"Two Shirley Temples," Randall called.

"You idiot, those are non-alcoholic."

"Oh, right. Waitress! Two white Russians."

While they waited, Stone said, "Hey you know who else is a white Russian?"

"Rocky?" said Randall. "No, wait, the other guy."

"That chick who wanted to bang Nardo. Remember her?"

"Dude, all Russians are white."

"What the hell was her name? Svetlana? Ivanna?"

"Oh! I remember! Ilyana."

"Barista Ilyana. You know what I'm going to do?" said Stone. The white Russians appeared in front of them. "I'm going to get Nardo laid."

"I'd like to see that! I mean, how are you going to achieve this wonder?" Not all of these words were pronounced clearly, but they got the point across.

Stone had his phone out. He was logging into Twitter. After a search or two he found @barista_Ilyana, and drunkenly typed out the message: "I know you want to bang nardo you can find him at the pizza king on north street pretty much all day good luck he has the clap." He started laughing and finally, after much consideration, deleted the clap part before sending. Give the guy a break. He finished his white Russian and called for two martinis.

"Nardo said you said Twitter was for homos," Randall pointed out afterwards.

Stone snorted. "I just don't give a shit about his boring-ass wrestling."

"Oh."

"Shoot me in the head if I ever have to look at his feed again."

It was April seventh.

6 It is impossible to kill your wife. It's *possible*, of course, but you'll always get caught. The same is true for a husband, or a girlfriend. You don't have to watch too many true crime specials to figure that out.

Carol was fond of a particular loose-leaf tea, which she bought in little pressed cakes and brewed in a special infuser Colin had bought her—one infuser for her house, one for his. The tea cake expanded in hot water, blossoming into a large hunk of tea leaves.

Let's say Colin had been busy rewiring a lamp and he happened to leave the exposed cord plugged in on the hardwood floor. Say he made some tea for a still sleeping Carol and set it on the edge of the night stand, then left to get bagels.

Such was his inexperience that he'd put too many tea cakes in the infuser, though —three or four—and filled it with hot water to the brim. While he was out of the house, the tea cakes would expand. They'd displace the water and the brewing tea would overflow the infuser and flow down to the floor…connecting the current between the cord and the metal bed frame of Colin's bed. Since Carol usually slept with her head pillowed on her biceps, her hand stretched above her head and resting against (Colin had noticed) the metal bars of the metal headboard…

Was that enough current to kill someone? How could you ever look up whether it was enough current to kill someone without implicating yourself? Would it be clear that the time of death happened while Colin was away? Would the whole thing even look like an accident? Would Colin be considered so irresponsible that his act would be criminal anyway?

No, there was no way to kill Carol Wernick. And yet her concerned visits would have to stop if Colin was going to get anything done.

Colin had spent the weekend keeping the same schedule as Friday: ten fifteen to five at Sunset Grove. He shared a lunch with mother and then left just before dinner. They passed the day watching her stories in the TV room, or playing cards "with the girls."

"What's all this attention for?" she asked, flattered.

"I just had some time off, mom."

But he told the staff some canned stories of forgetfulness. "Maybe it's no big deal," he admitted.

"We'll keep an eye on her," the Jamaican nurses promised.

When he came back from Salton, Carol would come over with dinner. It was actually useful, telling her about the day, because it reinforced the little fibs he'd fed the staff and made them more "real" and therefore easier to remember. But if she kept this up—the plan did not accommodate her keeping this up.

Breaking up with her would probably be just as bad as killing her—the whole point was to create a pattern and not deviate from it, and ending a relationship was by definition a deviation. Instead, Sunday night he acted distraught. He sent her home fairly early, balancing concern that she needed to be at work tomorrow with a desire to be alone with his worry. He figured the next day he could get her to stay away for a few days, enough time for his Monday and Tuesday night plans; and then, in case he was tired Wednesday night, Wednesday night, too.

After she left he did the laundry—*the* laundry. He sat with his white board for a while. There really was no way to kill her or dump her. When the drier buzzed, Colin went down in the basement.

He opened the drier, to make sure the clothes truly were dry, but then realized if he touched them the whole reason for washing them could be compromised. He didn't want any oil from his skin getting deposited on the material.

Of course, he was going to have to *wear* the clothes. But with the exception of the gloves, nothing in the drier would end up touching his skin—he'd have a full suit of clothes underneath. Colin squatted a moment in front of the drier's open mouth, trying to figure if this caution was rational. Finally he stuck an elbow in. It all felt dry. Even if an elbow was not so sensitive, even if the clothes were a little wet, surely they would dry in the two days they were scheduled to sit there.

Colin left the clothes, pulled out the lint filter, and peeled the lint off. He put the lint in a plastic bag, and then scraped the filter with a paper towel. This just generated more lint, as the paper towel started to disintegrate, so Colin washed the filter off thoroughly. He took the bag full of lint with him, the next morning, as he drove to see his mother. He stopped at that rest stop off I-81 to use the bathroom. The lint went in a garbage can there.

He'd have to fix the Carol problem tonight. He regretted not having it checked off yet.

7 Hunter Arnoux spent all weekend brooding about what he referred to as *opportunity*. "Opportunity" was his pet term for a crisis, because of something he'd once read, or more likely heard. He was afraid of an opportunity.

The opportunity was one Colin Lang. Like most people, Arnoux considered himself a good judge of when someone was lying; unlike most people, Arnoux had a proven track record. Something in Colin's excuse about seeing his mother stuck in Arnoux's craw—especially the part where he asked to go and then put it off. Why would someone so worried about his mother that he wanted a week off from work not "jump at the chance" of leaving right away? Why would Lang want to "put one over" on Hunter Arnoux? There was only one possibility.

Colin Lang was applying to other jobs.

It made sense! Arnoux didn't really understand how someone with the obvious drive and charisma of a Colin Lang had been overlooked for more promotions for so long. Arnoux would prioritize correcting the oversight—was he not an overseer? But certainly a proactive achiever like Lang would start "taking the law into his own hands." Arnoux should have done something to grease Lang's palm long ago. YOU SNOOZE YOU LOSE read the poster in Arnoux's private office; and Arnoux had snost and lost.

He'd just have to deduce what companies Lang was shopping himself out to, and somehow "poison the well." Such a deduction would have been practically impossible, except "the walls have ears" and Arnoux remembered the scuttlebutt about Lang and a certain Miss Carol Wernick.

At this point, Arnoux silently reminded himself that saying "poisoning the well" was considered antisemitic, so he shut the whole thought process down.

Until Monday. On Monday his little plan took effect. He casually visited the third floor and casually walked past Carol Wernick's desk.

"Oh," he said. "Carol…Wernick? Right?"

Yes, of course, so he introduced himself.

"We've actually met several t—" she began, but Arnoux had a spiel prepared.

"You know my boy Colin Lang, don't you?" he said.

"Yes, we're…dating?" She clearly looked afraid. Probably thought he was a narc, come to "harsh her buzz."

"Lang. That's not a Chinese name, is it?"

"No, he's not Chinese."

"He took a week off, you know. Do you know where he's going on vacation?"

"He...he's looking after his mother. He didn't really go anywhere. I mean, she lives in Salton, but he's just commuting."

"Oh, come now, Carol, Carol. We both know he's not going to Salton. We both know what's really going on."

But no amount of cajole or bluster could worm anything else out of her. Arnoux harrumphed back to his private office. He sat in his large chair, "literally stewing." He would prove that there was no mother, no charitable visits. This was not Philadelphia, the city of maternal love: this was Cottinend, and Mr. Arnoux would not be fooled! He pressed the speaker on his phone.

"Cathy, get me Sunset Rest Funeral Home in Salton. Ask for Colin Lang; he should be there visiting his mother, presumably a Mrs. Lang."

"I'm sorry, sir, did you say Sussaruss Utero in Ellen?"

"Sunset Rest! Sunset Rest Funeral Home! Ask for Colin Lang."

"Asher cling clang?"

In a rage, Hunter Arnoux actually picked *up the phone*, like a *goddamn plebeian*, and spelled out very slowly the precise details of what he needed. It turned out that there was no Sunset Rest Funeral Home in Salton, but there was a Sunset Grove Senior Living Facility, and obviously that was what he meant.

While he waited, the stupid phone against his ear, to be connected *and proved right*, he said, "You cannot have a hunt without a Hunter."

"Hello," a voice said at last. "This is Colin."

Arnoux was completely flummoxed. "Colin! Colin, hello! This is Hunter Arnoux. I completely expected to reach you there. I was just wondering, the Meniscus file—did you save it on the J: or K: drive?"

"I saved it on my desktop," the voice said.

"Just so. Perfect. Enjoy your...mother." He hung up quickly.

"I'll be good goddamned," thought Arnoux. "An honest man!"

8 Carol thought her run-in with Mr. Arnoux was nothing more than a confusing, amusing little story she'd tell Colin and laugh about later. But then, when she called him after work to see if he'd be home soon, to see if she could swing by, he sounded strange. He suggested that he needed some time to process his emotions and think about what he'd have to do about his mother.

"Are you breaking up with me?" Carol asked, sitting in her car.

"What? No. I just need a few days alone. I'll call you on Thursday or Friday, that's all."

The request almost seemed reasonable, and Carol could see herself asking for something similar if her own mother had been having problems. But for it to come after Arnoux's insinuation. What if Colin wasn't going to Sunset Grove? What if his mother wasn't suffering cognitive decline? She'd sounded fine on the phone with Carol!

"Can I...can I call you?" She knew it was wheedling. Did she hear him sigh over the line?

"It's just that..."

"I mean," she said, "in case something comes up. A work emergency." She tried to recover some of her dignity. "Perhaps I'd have to call your mother's room at Sunset Grove?"

There was hesitation, and he stressed that he wouldn't get to his mother's until quarter after ten, but he did give Carol the direct number, which was something.

Carol made dinner for one and sat in front of the TV with it and vowed she wouldn't call or even think of Colin until the end of the week. She was already seething with self-contempt because she knew it was a vow she would break.

9 Sp!der should have seen the message earlier, but so many gentlemen sent randy messages to Ilyana Petranova that two days went by before he suspected one of those messages had a more serious import. He was scrolling through her Twitter notifications during an after-dinner snack when it hit him.

Everyone wants to bang Ilyana and everyone thinks she wants to bang them—
who writes saying Ilyana wants to bang a third person? *Nardo at the Pizza King on
North Street is who.*

On a hunch he quickly googled it up, and indeed, Cottinend had a Pizza King
on North Street. Plenty of other places did, too, but this was the best lead he had
so far. All he needed to do was call the Cottinend Pizza King and ascertain who
Nardo was. According to google they were still open for another two hours.

Several ways to play it, Sp!der thought, psyching himself up for his first
phone call in weeks. He could play it smooth and worm the information out of
them before they even knew what was happening. Or he could play it forceful,
masterfully overpower them. They'd have no choice but to tell him what he
needed. Or he'd lie, pretending to be a...a contest chairman. "We need Nardo's
full name and address to process his claim."

Sp!der decided on smooth and dialed the number. He breathed deeply as it
rang, calming himself. Smooth.

But then a woman's voice answered, and instead of *hello* she said, "Pizza King.
We're not taking any more orders tonight."

Sp!der was immediately flustered—at least in part by the sudden realization
that because of time zones Pizza King would be closing in less than ten minutes;
but also because it was a woman's voice. Abruptly he switched to masterful. "Listen here!" he barked. "You will tell me the full name of any Nardo or Nardos that
work at this establishment."

"Get lost, asshole. I'm blocking this number."

Sp!der began to explain that there was no point in blocking this number; he
would simply route his calls through a server in Estonia and it would appear as a
different number each time. But before he got very far into the explanation she'd
hung up.

"I probably should have lied," Sp!der thought, as he redialed. Time to take a
different tack. But to his horror, he shunted right to voice mail. His number really

was blocked. How could they do this to him? He had no idea how to route a call through Estonia!

One thing, he could call John Oberman and get him to go to Pizza King. But then he wouldn't be delivering the answer all tidily wrapped. The fame and the glory wouldn't be his. He needed to call Pizza King back!

Sp!der huffed up the stairs. "Ma! I need to use the phone!"

"Go ahead, sweetie. It's free."

"I mean long distance." The landline was locked for long distance after Sp!der had conducted a brief flirtation with a woman from the Philippines. She turned out not to be, in fact, a woman, but the part about the Philippines was true, and it only did not turn out worse because Sp!der had already lost his credit card privileges after an earlier flirtation—that was when his cell phone had been blocked for international calls. After the Philippines debacle his mother had gone ahead and blocked not just international but *all* long distance calls from the land line. That was *five years ago*, but still only his mother had the code.

"Who are you going to call?" his mother shouted from the other room, her voice half-drowned out by the soundtrack of musical "stings" coming from the television. It was some CNN mockumentary. Sp!der had his own news sources, and he was about to tell his mother off for listening to propaganda news, and for saying *who* instead of *whom*, when he remembered that he needed her help. Furthermore, he needed to answer the question she had just asked.

And this was a pickle for Sp!der. He could hardly say he wanted to call a pizza parlor in New York State. He could hardly explain why he needed to do this. He stood there with his mouth open, one hand on the useless phone, while his mother shouted,

"Who's it, Mickey? Who you calling, Mickey?"

And then he had a brainwave. "Ronnie, ma!"

Veronica was his cousin, which meant she would have to take a call from him. Actually, that wasn't true; her house phone had caller ID, and she would never answer a call from Sp!der's cell; but if he called from the landline, Ronnie would assume it was Sp!der's mother calling, and pick up. The fact that Sp!der's mother knew this added a dollop of plausibility to the plan. And it wasn't even a lie. His mother would go through he phone bills; she would see he called Ronnie's house.

"Oh, how nice, going to call your cousin," Sp!der's mother said as she shuffled into the room. While Sp!der ostentatiously turned his back, she typed in the passkey. Then for good measure she dialed Ronnie's Florida number and handed the phone to Sp!der as it started to ring. Then it was back to CNN with her, to learn to see the world through corporate media's eyes.

Fortunately Ronnie and not her idiot husband answered. "Auntie Carmen? What's up."

"Ronnie? It's me, Michael. Don't hang up!"

"Agh! Give me one good reason why I shouldn't hang—"

"Because I need a favor," Sp!der said.

"That's not a very compelling—"

But now Sp!der was just lying to family. This part he had practice in; this part was easy.

"Look, you'd be doing a good deed. I have a friend, a young woman, and I'm afraid she might be in danger."

"You do not have a friend who is a young—"

"She's not so very young. She was a neighbor back when I lived in upstate New York. She plays Warhammer 40k." Sp!der could hear it, he could hear Ronnie drawing breath to say, "I have no idea what that is," so he powered through before she could. "She met this guy, and she only knows his first name and where he works; and I just need to learn his last name so I can do an internet search about him, make sure he's not some kind of criminal."

"Why on earth—"

"Come on, she's been hurt before."

"Why on earth," Ronnie said again, "would you be doing this for a girl, assuming she's real?"

And this was where Sp!der had her. He knew he could count on her contempt. "Ronnie," he said, "have you ever heard the word *friendzone*?"

It took a little more, but finally she produced a gurgling sigh and said, "All right."

"Great! I can give you the number."

She fumbled for a pen and jotted it down. "What time to they close?" she asked.

He looked at the microwave clock. "Uh...yeah, they're already closed."

"Fine, I'll do it tomorrow. What's his name?"

"Nardo at Pizza King in Cottinend. It's right near where we used to live. Do you remember that house? You and Greg came—"

"Mickey, I've got to go. I'll text you his name tomorrow."

"No, wait!" Sp!der knew that John had said no texts, no emails, but that wasn't what he was worried about. He just didn't want to give up the chance for another phone call. "My phone bricked, you need to call this number."

"Fine, fine."

"Have a great—"—but she had already hung up.

Sp!der stood for a moment, wondering idly if he'd pork his cousin, like maybe if she wasn't his cousin. After weighing all the pros and cons, he decided she was probably getting too old. He headed back downstairs. He wished he'd had more time to stress to Ronnie how important her mission was. Nevertheless, he was feeling proud of the work he had done. He should call Oberman and tell him that the case was almost closed. But, much as he hated to avoid a phone call, he knew if he got through to Oberman, Oberman would just grill him on all the details, on why the case was *almost closed* and not *fully closed*. He'd use his cop techniques to get the truth from him, and the truth made Sp!der look a little bit like an idiot.

Therefore: Sp!der started texting Oberman, in direct contravention of Oberman's explicit instructions. He started texting while still on the stairs, missed the last step, and almost bobbled his phone. He plopped down in his swivel chair before he finished the text, which was, he thought, vague enough not to violate Oberman's directive.

He wrote: "The cat is in the bag. More news tomorrow."

Only after he sent it did he realize that cats came out of bags, not into bags, and he meant that the investigation was in the bag. He felt embarrassed to have sent something so stupid.

"I mean it's all figured out except the final confirmation," he wrote then.

And Oberman texted back, "Call me." So Sp!der shut off his phone.

It was April ninth.

10 Near the Ridgemont Rest assisted living facilities on Ridgemont Road, Route 434, stands a sad, decaying twenty-four hour diner. Some three miles away is a Polish-themed old-man pub. Everything else on the strip closes early. Manicurist, aquarium supply, tot lot: They all close before seven; the supermarket closes at eight; Choice Pizza, over by the pub, stays open till nine on weekdays, or at least it did before it shut down for good. This is before it shut down: right before it shut down. The night of April ninth.

On that night Colin Lang took his car out into his driveway, just to get a little more room. In the garage he turned his bicycle upside down. He spread a garbage bag under it like a tarp.

They had shown him, when he bought the bicycle, were the serial number was. He'd considered filing it off months ago, but had figured that there were still so many things that could happen—the bike could get swiped or impounded or just looked over by a policeman. Surely a bike without a serial number appeared to be stolen! He left the filing to the last minute. Perhaps the removal of the numbers wasn't strictly necessary, as nothing should ever connect the bicycle with the Incident. But no harm in being careful. He turned the bike back over, and folded the corners of the garbage bag up, gathering the filings. He put that bag into another garbage bag and put it in his pocket, along with a bandana, still in the original plastic wrap. He checked his pockets to make sure he had a wallet but no cell phone. He checked the combination lock to make sure it was open and set correctly—*159*—but wedged tight on the chain so it would not fall off as he rode. He checked and then triple checked inside the handlebars to make sure no paper had been left there. He checked to make sure the car was locked—he'd leave it in the driveway. Wearing gloves he wiped the whole bike down. Only then did he hop on and begin the long ride to Ridgemont Road.

It wasn't actually a long ride, only five miles or so, but a lot of it was uphill. This was the foothills of the Appalachian Mountains, and all of Cottinend slopes uphill, south to north. The night was dark and overcast. Colin had a light on the front of his bike, and a flashing red light on the back of his seat. Even under the sherpa hat, his ears were cold.

A mirror on his handlebars would light up periodically as a car's headlights crept up behind him. In an explosion of brightness, the car would speed past. One or two angry drivers leaned on the horn, either to warn him they were coming or just out of annoyance. Some of these streets were not the kind cyclists usually frequented.

When he reached a street with a short stretch of sidewalk, he pulled over and removed the garbage bag from his pocket. He could feel the cold wind on his face even while stopped. When no cars were coming he dumped out the metal filings making sure to stand upwind. He shook both bags. Whatever came off them was invisible in the night. Then he rode on. The first trash can he passed got the two garbage bags. He kept on, uphill.

This would have been easier, Colin estimated, ten years ago, when he was younger. A light rain started up.

Finally, huffing a little, Colin pulled over onto a little grass margin of Ridgemont Road and turned off both his lights. Nearly blind he pedaled the final twenty yards to the rainslick darkened parking lot of Choice Pizza. Hopping off his bike he groped his way forward. He'd thought the night was dark along the road, but behind the pizza place it was dark like the back of a closet. He found himself completely disoriented and had to turn his handlebar light on to find where he was. Keeping it mostly off, he managed by touch to locate the metal dumpster. The side of the dumpster was so cold it radiated through his leather glove. He popped the light off the handlebars and used it as a flashlight, locating the handle he'd seen. He threaded the chain around it, passed it through the front tire and the bike frame, and closed the combination lock. He had practiced this move in the dark, but he used the bike light anyway, just in case. With his thumb he dialed back the third digit of the lock. *158*.

Now came the hard part. He wished it weren't raining. Holding the bike light in one hand, trying not to get completely muddy, he scrambled up the embankment. It was easier than he'd feared. He hurried through the woods, pausing to pick up a sturdy stick, until he could see the streetlights along Blande Boulevard. The bike light went off. There were no cars.

Quickly, Colin ripped the red bandana free from its plastic wrap, which he stuck in his pocket. He tied the bandana to a stick he found, and broke from the tree cover. Right where the trail started, right along the side of the road, Colin jammed the stick into the ground. He worried it in deeper until shifting lights indicated a car coming. He didn't want to hit the deck—he'd be covered in filth— so he retreated to behind a tree. After the car passed he came back and forced the stick down until it was sunk too deep even to wiggle.

Back through the woods using the bike light sparingly. It was actually good practice to follow the trail again, after so long. Down the embankment. Once in the parking lot, he put the bike light in his jacket pocket for the walk back toward the road. Facing Ridgemont, the blackness was not quite so pitch; it was easier to head that way without stumbling. He stopped under a streetlight to see how dirty he was. His shoes, and the bottom of his pants were bad, and one glove, but the rest was wet without looking like a ditch digger. He walked along the dark road for a few minutes until he came to Krakow Nights.

The pub really was a sleepy affair. Old men sat hunched over the tables. They stuck their feet straight out, a series of trip hazards, and their socks were checkered and pulled up high and tight. Colin figured he might as well have a good time if he was already out on the town, so he ordered a whiskey sour and headed to the bathroom. He washed his hands, but he spent more time rinsing off his glove, and cleaning his shoes and legs with paper towels.

The drink was waiting for him when he returned. "You looked pleased with yourself," the bartender said.

Colin considered telling her that he was nearing the end of a project, but decided that was risking too much. "I'm on a staycation," he said.

"Did you walk here?" she asked, nodding towards his soggy hair.

Colin shrugged. "Pub crawl," he said. She smiled big, and he set his cash on the bar. It included a five-dollar tip. He'd need her on his side. He finished his drink and called for another. Alcohol didn't usually do it for him, but he was feeling all right. Foreign music played low in the background. This was the quietest bar Colin had ever been in. He liked it.

Nursing his whiskey, Colin leaned on the bar and scanned the room. He had to be the youngest person in the place. Actually, the bartender had to be the youngest. He looked back and she was smiling at him. He knew she had to flirt with customers to get a tip, but he was still getting a serious energy off her.

The bartender set a third whiskey in front of him. "On the house," she said.

She was probably too young for him, Colin thought, but not so young that you'd have to be embarrassed by it. She looked good, in the way that younger people seem to when you get older. The spray of freckles across the bridge of her nose was charmingly out of place; she wasn't as fair as freckled people usually looked She certainly didn't look Polish. If it wasn't for Carol, he decided, he'd probably go for it. He sipped his free drink.

But then he realized: He was less than two days away from the most audacious Incident in…was it fair to say in American history? In any event, it seemed almost hypocritical to worry about conventional mores such as fidelity in the shadow of such an Incident.

And he was about to turn around. He was about to ask her about when she got off.

When he realized (a second time) that the one thing he must not do was *anything unusual*. It was folly to even be in the bar. He hadn't been solo at a bar since that night in October. Already he was forming an excuse, if anyone asked him where he'd been that night. He was just so worried about his mother; a nightcap for worry.

He still turned around, but all he said to the cute bartender and her freckles was, "Could you do me a favor, call me a cab? I'm a little tipsy."

"You sure?" she asked. But it was a request no bartender could turn down. She was already reaching for the bar phone.

Colin finished his drink while looking out the window. The rain had gotten worse. When the cab's headlights pulled up, Colin put a thank-you twenty on the bar.

"In another lifetime," he said to her, wistfully.

"What?" she said.

The cab took him to an address near his house. He paid cash and watched its tail lights disappear before he walked home through the rain.

11 Carol lay in bed not sleeping. She felt pathetic for thinking so much about a silly thing. She always felt pathetic when she spent too much time thinking about a boy, about Colin, and what else had she thought about these last three months? Was her life really this small that she couldn't spend two or three days without him around?

It was past midnight, so she probably shouldn't call him. She *definitely* shouldn't call him, anyway, but it was rude to call past midnight. She texted instead, just a *thinking about you*. Then she called. There was no response.

The stupidest thing to do would be to go to his house.

He was almost certainly sleeping after all. She couldn't let herself in because she didn't have a key. Was it weird that she didn't have a key?

Even if he was sleeping, she certainly was not. There was no harm in her driving past his house. She could look at his house. If a light was on downstairs, only then would she knock on the door.

She told herself this was a stupid idea, but she already had flats and an overcoat on. She already had her keys in her hand.

There was, indeed, a light on in his living room. His car was in the driveway, which was only slightly unusual—he tended to put it in the garage, but sometimes, on clear nights, he kept it out.

It was not a clear night.

Carol parked behind his car. She knocked at his door, then rang the doorbell. No answer, so she slipped behind a shrubbery and peeked through the window. The TV was on, but she couldn't see anyone there. Had he fallen asleep on the couch?

Suddenly embarrassed that she'd come, Carol scurried back to her car. She winced when the motor caught—surely he had heard it, surely he was waking up. She just wanted to get home before anyone knew she'd left.

She'd pulled out of the driveway and had rounded a corner when she saw in her headlights a man paying a cab. She knew at a glance that the man was Colin Lang. She drove by with her shoulders hunched up, although of course her face would be invisible in the dark car anyway. Either Colin had looked up and recognized her license plate or he hadn't. And based on what she could make out in her rear view mirror he hadn't.

A few houses down Carol stopped and backed into a driveway. Her heart was hammering. There was nothing particularly strange about taking a cab home—she'd never known Colin to do it, but it wasn't crazy. Why didn't he take the cab all the way home, though? Why did he get out a block away? She waited until that self-same cab drove past her and then she pulled out of the driveway and tailed it. This, she thought, was absurd. And yet she did it; it was ridiculously easy to follow a pair of tail lights along the dark empty streets. She tailed the cab until it hit a stoplight on Scenic Heights. She pulled up behind;

immediately, Carol hopped out of the car, leaving the door open and ran through the rain to the cab. She knocked on the widow.

The cabby looked scared as he rolled the window down. Carol could hardly be mistaken for a robber; was he afraid she was going to complain about his driving to his manager?

"It's okay," she said, trying to smile big, trying to look friendly. "I just had a question."

The man smiled back, but it the smile was a rictus of fear. He was a Sikh. Maybe he was a foreigner; maybe he was concerned she was going to try to deport him.

"That last fare you had. Right back there? I just wanted to know where you picked him up."

"Krakow Nights, lady." And of course at first she thought he'd said, "Krakow, nice lady," like Jerry Lewis confessing he'd driven from Poland. But then she remembered that it was a bar.

Back in her car, and then back in her bed, she worried that maybe she'd forgotten to thank the cabby, or even maybe she should have tipped him. But mostly she worried about Colin Lang. Even if it was not ridiculous to go out to a bar when worried about a loved one, and then to take a cab home like a responsible drinker—none of this was like him.

She did not necessarily vow that she would stake him out the next night and see what was up, but she knew, on a deeper level, that she was going to be doing it. And only then could she fall asleep.

12 Bernie was up at dawn. He looked out the window and corrected himself. He was up before dawn. ¶ Some part of him remembered the day he'd jumped Alan Jancewicz, so many years ago. He'd had a fantasy, before he'd done it, that the act would make him popular. That the next day he'd come to school and the whole school would be gathered, laughing and chatting.

When he arrived, everyone would cheer, and want to slap his hand. The girls would giggle nervously.

It didn't go that way, of course. He was a laughingstock because he'd lost, but some part of him, over the years, had come to understand that he would have been worse off if he had won. It had been a trap! If Alan beat up Bernie, then Bernie was a joke; if Bernie beat up Alan, then Bernie was a villain.

This was so unfair it only made Bernie hate Alan more! Just thinking about the trap got Bernie feeling angry again.

But he was dimly aware, only deep deep down but still aware that there was some relevance to his current situation, and he might have had time to stop and think and figure out what it was if he wasn't so busy waiting for the sun to sidle up and the great day to begin.

13 John Oberman had the early shift that week, which sounded worse than it was. He had to be at work by seven, but he got off at 3:30. ¶ He woke up on April tenth expecting the news to be full of some atrocity, but everything was quiet. This was good! It meant he wasn't too late. The Sp!der could call at any moment. Everything could fall into place

The quiet smiles of his compatriots Oberman bore stoically. He could hear them suppressing a chuckle as he walked by. "If nothing happens they are going to roast me alive," Oberman thought.

Campbell suppressed nothing. "Where's your damned massacre?" he had asked first thing when Oberman picked him up, and he asked it again after roll call.

"Pray God nothing happens," Oberman said.

"Well, somewhere in Bangladesh…" Campbell started. But then they were driving past the fire station, so Campbell angrily rolled down his window and threw a lit cigarette at the station house. It bounced around on the driveway. "Fucking losers," he said. "Anyway, mark my words, somewhere in Cottinend, Bangladesh, or somewhere like that, you'll see a Muslim bombing on the news and it'll all fall into place."

14 He wore work shoes, but then he always wore work shoes when he went to see his mother. She liked him to dress "nicely." He took Blande, of course, and he noted, as he went, that last night's red bandana still waved.

15 Amber hung up the Pizza King's phone. She had always pitied Bernie, but now—she knew his parents were dead, but here his beloved aunt had died and no one knew how to reach him. His cousin called just to get his address, which of course Amber didn't know. She had a cell number—all the employees passed them around in case they needed to swap shifts, but the cousin was oddly uninterested. All Amber could tell her was to look up Bernard Feldstein in Cottinend. It seemed so sad.

Maybe, she thought, the death and his grief explained why Bernie wasn't at work today. But that didn't make any sense—how would he know before his cousin called? And anyway, she remembered now that Mr. Prishtine had said that Bernie had phoned out, that he was just very drunk.

One thing Amber was not was suspicious. The cousin had referred to Bernie by the same name Bernie's friends did, when they came by the pizza place, before Mr. Prishtine'd kick them out. She called him *Nardo*.

16 It was a quiet day. Oberman kept jumping at every little radio squawk and Campbell sighed like a bellows each time. By three o'clock, everyone had their little smirks.

"Still plenty of day left, Johnny," Lepage said. "You might still get lucky."

17 Sp!der called Ronnie and got her husband and then he called her again and left a message on the machine and again until his mother stopped agreeing to type in the code for him. "She'll call you back, Mickey."

"She's not really out, ma! Her husband's lying."

"She'll call you back when she's ready. She's probably just working late."

"Do you know her cell phone number, ma? She'd get that at work."

"Oh, I never can keep straight all these fool cell phone numbers…"

"Okay, fine. Well, do you know where she works?"

But she didn't. Fat lot she knew.

18 Carol knew that Colin would not be getting back home from mother's until after six. She drove to his house right after work and circled the block, looking for a place to spy from. Finally she decided her best bet was to park a few blocks away and then hide herself across the street from Colin's house in a little copse of trees. In the dark she should be invisible both to Colin, in his house or his car, and—just as importantly—to whoever owned this copse.

Of course, dusk wouldn't be for another couple of hours. She drove home and ate dinner. She packed a few energy bars and a thermos of coffee. She got her warmest coat, just in case the night got cold. She was going to figure this out once and for all.

And she did all this without thinking too hard about it. Because if she'd thought about it she would have stopped. It was ridiculous. If his secret was that he went to a bar now and then alone, this was a small secret.

But of course, all this time Carol had been banking on the notion that Colin only had deep secrets.

Around dusk she came back to his house. The lights were on, although the car must have been, as usual, in the garage. She parked around the corner and snuck in the gloaming around to the trees. She settled down, preparing for a long boring wait.

She was prepared for everything but what she saw.

19 Colin went outside, unlocked the side door of his garage, and went back into his house. With the electric razor he made a final pass over his knuckles, the backs of his hands, his wrists. Then he took a long shower, with exfoliant. Once out, he brushed his hair, then his eyebrows and eyelashes. If he could avoid leaving any DNA anywhere, this would be best.

Colin stood in his kitchen in a robe drinking a last cup of coffee. It smelled crisper and brighter than any cup he remembered having in a long time. It tasted so good he didn't wait for it to cool sufficiently, and of course he burned his tongue.

Finally he took out a Post-it pad and wrote a note in big block letters with a Sharpie. He peeled off the top sheet and put it in his pocket. Then as always, he removed a half-dozen more sheets. He took these and his junior disguise kit to the bathroom where he tore the extra Post-it sheets into tiny pieces. He flushed the tiny pieces down the toilet, adding a couple extra flushes. They went down fine. He'd been meaning to do a test like that for a while now; he knew if the paper didn't flush well he could always, when the time came, eat it.

Now, looking in the bathroom mirror, he built up his nose with putty and stuck on a thin mustache. He took his time. It should look natural. Then he brushed his teeth; it was early for it—quarter after eight—but there'd be no opportunity to brush later.

He removed his car key from the ring. The top of the key was large and plastic, and threading it off the ring took a while, but when he was done, he washed the car key off and wiped it down—probably unnecessary, but you never could tell—and, holding it with a tissue, set the key on his kitchen counter. The rest of the ring he hung up by the door, where it usually went. His watch was on the counter nearby.

After fetching his pair of pliers from the garage, he unlocked the basement door and went downstairs to the clothes drier. With the pliers he pushed aside the larger items until he found a left leather glove. It looked a little duller than usual. Probably shouldn't put leather through the wash, Colin thought.

He eased the glove on with the pliers and flexed his hand. It still fit fine, which was important. He wouldn't be taking it off for twelve hours or so.

With both gloves on he removed a pair of coveralls and a duffel bag from the drier and put the former in the latter. Then he took out the other coveralls and put them on, zipping them up carefully. He had transferred the Post-it from pants pocket to coveralls. The rest of the drier's load—a windbreaker and a scarf—went in the duffel bag as well. He carried both the duffel bag and the gym bag with the rifle in it upstairs and laid them on the kitchen floor, where no identifying carpet fibers could get on them. He realized he was still holding the pliers, so he set them on the floor, too, where they'd be out of the way. Out of the duffel came the broken-in hiking boots, and he put them next to the bags. The windbreaker and scarf on top of the boots.

Colin walked back to the bathroom in his stocking feet and fitted the blond wig on. He looked ridiculous. Then he inserted the cotton to puff out his cheeks. Sure, he looked even more ridiculous, but he didn't look like himself. He picked up a plunger and started plunging the toilet. No telltale scraps of colored paper came floating up. Everything was going fine.

There was plenty of time for a final check. The gym bag had a tricked-out rifle and nothing else. The duffel bag held (roughly top to bottom):

- One roll of packing tape.
- A cylinder of sterile wipes.
- A couple extra black plastic garbage bags.
- A Ziploc baggie with the burner phone and the battery.
- Two cheese sandwiches and a banana wrapped up in a grocery flier he'd grabbed off the street.
- A pair of black coveralls.
- Two Alfred E. Neuman masks, slightly mutilated.
- One piece of cardboard, cut down, creased on one edge, and, although formerly white, shaded in black with a Sharpie; a length of black thread was coiled up and taped on the back.
- Four VHS holders.
- Four times seven equals twenty-eight magazines, plus two spares for a total of thirty.
- A concomitant number of bullets.

Colin realized that he'd meant to pick up a small scissors somewhere secure, and had forgotten. He thought about wiping off one he owned, and decided against it. He could do without.

He put on the windbreaker. The scarf went in the jacket pocket. The car key went in the pocket of the coveralls, along with the wallet. He made a last walk through to make sure that the house was staged properly: some but not all lights illuminated; the TV loud.

With the help of the shoehorn, he wriggled the boots on and laced them tight. Now came another problem. He considered bringing the shoehorn along, just in case he had to take a boot off and put it back on. But he had not thought it out before; he had not carefully considered whether there was anything about the shoehorn that might identify him, nor had he thought up a cover story about why he needed to be carrying a shoehorn. Finally he put it in his coveralls pocket, planning to move it to the glove compartment when he got to the car.

Suddenly Colin had a memory: of when he was a child, and in late August his friends and he would be dreading the coming school year. They knew that time passed quickest when one was doing stuff, and slowest when one was bored; so they lay on the lawn and did nothing, just to make the summer last a little longer.

He stood for a moment in the kitchen and then exited through the patio door in back, leaving it unlocked. He had no house key on him, after all. Just as he left he heard his phone ring; it sounded, though the walls, so distant, and he decided to let it go. There was no dealing with Carol at this moment. He walked around the house to his garage. Entering through the unlocked side door, he hit the switch to winch the garage door, slowly, upwards. It felt like a curtain raising. He did not say, "showtime!" but the thought was there.

'Tis easier watching a night or two than to sit up a whole year together.
•Bunyan, *The Pilgrim's Progress* II (1684).

iv. ONE LONG NIGHT.

Colin Lang • Carol Wernick • Bernie Feldstein • Colin Lang • Carol Wernick • Bernie Feldstein • John Oberman • Colin Lang • Carol Wernick • Seamus Donofrio • Colin Lang • Bernie Feldstein • John Oberman • Colin Lang • Bernie Feldstein • Seamus Donofrio • Bernie Feldstein • Carol Wernick • Colin Lang • Cottinend, N.Y.

1 On April 10, a little after nine P.M., Colin Lang parked not at but near the all-night diner on Ridgemont. The street had, running along it, overflow parking spots that never got used, and Colin just pulled into one of those. If anyone asked he could say he was headed to the diner; it was hardly absurd for a diner patron to park here. He slipped his wallet out of his pocket, and the shoehorn fell out. He had been supposed to move the shoehorn to the glove compartment immediately upon entering the car! Colin cursed himself for making this error, but more for trying to improvise. He should have left the shoehorn at home! It was a stupid mistake, and he promised himself he would make no more of them. He opened the glove compartment and tucked the shoehorn in the back behind the registration. Then he put the wallet in as well, closer to the front, and closed the glove compartment.

That was a momentary hiccup. With the wallet put away everything was back on track.

Colin exited the car and locked it with the key, which was quieter than hitting the (*beep beep*) lock button. He walked past the diner. Then he kept walking along Ridgemont Road. The sidewalk disappeared, and he walked on the grassy margin. It felt weird not to have a watch, or phone, or any way to know the time. Still there was no need to hurry. Nothing relied on a precise schedule, at least not yet.

He didn't look like Colin Lang trudging along that deserted street, of course. The wig and the mustache; the nose putty and the cheek cotton. He had on the baseball cap he'd bought way back in November. It was a nondescript dark blue with a mesh back. He wore gloves and a windbreaker. The cotton scarf-end dangled from the jacket pocket. Something like a clunky bracelet ringed his wrist. The night was mild. There was a little moon, which was frankly a miracle in Cottinend, when the sky was usually too overcast for the sun, let alone the moon, to be seen. A car key was in his pants pocket, and a Post-it and a wadded black garbage bag, and nothing else.

An occasional car zoomed by, its headlights dazzling in the dark night. Unlike the Shopping District—designated as such by a series of twee signs built by the Rotarians—with its broad sidewalks bright lights and zebra crossings, the stores on Ridgemont Road were for drivers only. Colin walked past dark and empty lots. Sometimes he walked on the grass and sometimes he walked in the gutter. He walked for twenty minutes.

Ridgemont Rest had a short driveway with bushes and a flanking ornamental two-foot high brick wall, ringed by flood lights. Colin turned in, walking behind the flood lights. His feet crunched softly on the wood chips. The parking lot was much less well lit, a light-sink between the illuminated main building and the flood lights at the entrance. No one came or left the campus this late at night. Everyone was asleep, and the night nurses were probably playing poker. He stopped at a decorative border and picked up a rock the size of a cantaloupe.

Colin Lang had not hot-wired a car in three decades, but you never forget. He'd already returned to riding a bicycle. The only catch was that he needed an older car, one without the fancy computerized ignition. One unlike his own car. And here was a lot full of them.

The rock he wrapped in the scarf. He took the clunky bracelet off—it proved to be a roll of packing tape, the one he'd picked up at the Rite Aid in Ithaca. He stood next to an old beige station wagon—he didn't know much about cars, but it had to be from the 1980s. There was even a faded, half scraped-free Mondale bumper sticker: NDALE/RARO it read.

And this was the moment. Until now his only crime was the possession of an illegally modified illegal weapon. That was bad, but it was understandable. He could sell it to the judge: a fear for his life, encroaching lawlessness. He wouldn't lose his job over that one.

But once he put the rock through the window—no, once he put the packing tape on the window, everything would be different. Getting caught with packing tape on the widow would be hard to explain.

He pulled out a clear strip of packing tape. It made a *zetz* noise. He had no way to cut it, but he was prepared: He crouched and started breathing heavily through his mouth with his upper lip curled back. When his mouth was good and dry—no saliva, no DNA—he used his eye tooth to nick the tape, and took a strip off, then two, then three, four. Crisscrossed like an asterisk on the driver's side window, barely reflecting the slight moonlight, the tape strips made a target where they overlapped.

And, after all, he could run, and it was hard to imagine a security guard or a passerby chasing him down, in the pitch blackness. After all. Colin hefted the rock in the scarf. It was all very hard to explain.

Two minutes later, Colin had the car in neutral and he was pushing it towards the exit. The overhead light had only gone on for moment, when he opened the door, before he turned it off manually. One gloved hand on the window frame, one on the steering wheel—be careful not to hit the horn! He was very careful not to hit the horn. Once he judged himself close enough to the road, he slipped into the car and in the spent too many moments, a frightening number of moments— he was uncomfortably near the flood lights—fiddling under the dash in his gloves, before the engine sparked to life.

The scarf and the shattered window, its shards stuck together with packing tape, sat on the passenger seat. At the first light he pulled the trash bag from his pocket, and slipped them both in, followed by the roll of packing tape. The rock he'd carefully set down where it had been, at the margin of the lawn.

2 Carol had watched as the garage door opened and Colin's car pulled out. She should have stayed in her car, shouldn't she, to follow him when he drove away. She had no experience planning a stakeout!

But it wasn't Colin at the wheel. It was woman. Aha! So it was a woman after all. A blonde woman with a pageboy and a...

...and a mustache...

...and the blonde woman was Colin.

Oh my God, Carol thought. He's a transvestite!

She got up and walked to her car. She didn't know what to feel that wouldn't also be offensive in some way.

3 Since Bernie had started the morning of the tenth in a state of vibrating anticipation, every hour that passed since dawn had just been another metaphorical cup of coffee. Jangled is what his nerves did. When was this supposed to start? The scrap on the fridge just read: "apr 10" with no time stamp or anything.

He had called out from work, pretending he was sick. "I have really bad diarrhea and I think I saw blood and bits of hair in it," he'd told his boss. He went into a lot more crazy detail. Mr. Prishtine told him to just stay at home.

But what was there to do at home? The first thing was to dump all the garbage from the toter into the back yard. Then he rolled the toter to the front of the driveway. So that was done.

Next he had a few nervous beers, and then too many nervous beers, and then he passed out. When he woke up in the afternoon, he was afraid that his drunken stupor had made him miss Theodore Anderson's visit, and he resolved not to drink any more that day. He said this into the mirror, out loud, as he'd seen people do in movies, and as he looked himself in the eye and made his vow, he noticed that his hands were opening another beer. This would never do. He poured the beer down the toilet. Afterwards, he poured all his other beers down the toilet, seventeen of them. He went to see if he had any weed to put down the toilet, but he had so little he thought he might as well eat it. Then he got worried this was the wrong thing to do, so he tried to make himself throw up, unsuccessfully. He lay on the couch and wished he had some beer. He wished he had not deleted his Twitter account, but he was too scared to go open a new one.

He tried playing video games, but he just died, again and again, too quickly for it to be fun or even distracting. He was already distracted. Finally he put on the TV, but he couldn't watch it. The commercial jingles played

> *The best food in all New York*
> *Is Bagels-on-a-Fork!*

and they brought no solace. He sat on the staircase, halfway up, where he could look directly out the semicircular windows of the front door. He watched the driveway that no one came down.

No one came down and he watched and watched and was nevertheless taken entirely by surprise when the doorbell rang.

4 First thing Colin had done was drive the stolen car down the street to his own car. He parallel parked directly behind it—the street was so empty that practically this meant he just had to drive up and pull over and the two cars were a foot apart. No one was around to see Colin hop out of the still-idling car and open a trunk with a key. The trunk was lined with black plastic garbage bags, and sitting on those black garbage bags were a gym bag and that old duffel bag he'd found. Colin placed these into the stolen car, passenger side, and then closed the trunk quietly, putting his full weight on it to make it click; in a matter of seconds he was off, down the deserted street. He was going slow. He was using his turn signal. He did not drive towards Bernard Feldstein's house.

His first stop was Michaelson Road, at the point where the creek flowed through a pipe right under the road. It was called a creek, but in the spring it was more like a small river, four or five feet deep all the way to where it flowed into the Susquehanna. Colin just wanted to make sure it was full tonight. He pulled over and climbed out of the idling car, looking down over the low railing, but it was too dark to see the water. He walked over to where his headlights illuminated the roadside and picked up a glass beer bottle. He tossed it over the railing, and heard the splash. It sounded deep all right.

Back in the car, and next up was a Sarasota Avenue, a side street that connected two other side streets. Their garbage pickup, library research had told him, was tomorrow morning. Garbage toters sat at the end of every driveway, like sentries. Colin unfastened his seat belt as he drove, then pulled over to the left side of the street. His window was already down—or rather it was missing, but it *looked* like it was down—and in the dark he leaned out and dropped the garbage bag with the tape and the shattered window and the scarf into one almost-full toter. Nothing really suspicious about that. Just a motorist getting rid of some garbage in a socially responsible way. No litterbugging! He drove away, across town. Now he was driving toward's Bernard's.

Said Bernard lived on Coronet Street, a dead end not savvy enough to rebrand itself as a cul-de-sac. It was not a street Colin had even been down before. It was shaped like a comma.

Colin slowed along the curve. None of the houses had a garbage toter out, except one. He could see a car in the driveway, Pennsylvania plates. Bumper sticker hard to read. Headlights on the mailbox confirmed the address, the napkin address.

He drove to the end of the street, K-turned, and shut off his headlights, trusting to the moon. He unbuckled his seat belt and moved the two bags onto his lap. As he drove slowly back in the dark he veered over to the left side of the street. The looming shadow of the toter gave him a point to steer towards. Brake. Once again he was leaning out a window as he slid the bags into the garbage can. One thumped and one clattered, but they were quiet enough. Colin drove away, and hit the headlights again as he rounded the curve.

A short drive and one more turn, slowly and with a turn signal of course.

Rano Boulevard, you will recall, runs parallel to Coronet. Colin parked on Rano. He rolled down all the windows, one at a time, manually with a crank; the

110

rear windows only went down halfway. He left the car idling. With any luck it would be stolen in a couple of hours. Teenage Colin would have stolen it. Rano was a busy enough street; there must be teenagers there.

Now Colin wandered down Rano looking for a house with all the windows dark. Here! He walked up its side yard. He, Colin, must have been hard to see, or so he figured; maybe just a glint of blonde wig in the shadows. Once around the house in the backyard, he walked along, at a healthy distance from the rear of the house, moving from lot to lot. The backyards were dark. There were no fences between next-door neighbors here, or at most a low hedge he could step, or rather stumble, over. He also stumbled over gardens, sandboxes, patio chairs left out, cushionless, all winter. He hoped he was not leaving footprints, although probably it didn't matter. These boots were going in the trash tomorrow.

Despite all the barked shins and distractions, Colin was counting lots carefully, and he soon found himself in the very back of the back yard of one particular house. The house had a light on inside, the blue flickering ghostlight of a television set playing through a window; but it hardly reached where he was standing. Directly behind this house, their backyard's abutting was the home and person of Bernard Feldstein. By touch more than sight Colin found the low chain link fence that separated the two properties. As he had practiced so many times before, he put his hand on it, and vaulted. This was more difficult in the dark—he should have practiced it blindfolded, or at least with his eyes closed—and his foot caught. He spun in the air and landed with a thump that knocked the wind out of him.

"That was an oversight," he said, but silently. He subvocalized. "But that will be the last oversight." He stood up and brushed himself off. Bernie's house was all lit up, and he walked gingerly across an untidy backyard. There was one large and odorous pile of garbage: coffee grounds and wadded tissues and rotting food. Colin rolled his eyes at Bernard's resourcefulness. Then he was up three stairs to the rear door. An aluminum canopy shaded it from the eyes of heaven. Colin knocked on the window. There was no answer so he tried the knob.

"I should have told him to leave the back door open," Colin said, silently again. But Feldstein was always the hard part of the plan. Colin had barely had anything thought out when they'd met that one time at Munster, and it would never have done to initiate too many points of contact. This lapse was forgivable.

With a sigh more audible than his subvocalizations had been, Colin in the shadows rounded the house—there was no garage; the car, he noted, had no front plate—to ring from behind a shrubbery, only his arm extending out over the porch, the doorbell.

5 Carol thought she was just going to drive home, or to her parents's house to cry on her mother's shoulder, like a heroine from a 1940s melodrama. But she didn't drive home, or anywhere. She sat in her car, idly checking her phone, waiting for Colin to return.

Perhaps he was gay, as Aggie'd predicted, which might explain some things: the secrecy, the hidden depths. But then she kicked herself for confusing homosexuality with transvestism. If he was just a transvestite, off to a transvestite… bar? for transvestite…fun? This was worse, wasn't it? Somehow that felt like more of a betrayal, if only because she was less familiar with its implications. She'd known plenty of closeted gay men, back in the day; she'd known a couple of their aggrieved spouses. If she knew any closeted transvestites, she didn't know she knew them.

Then she thought he might not be a transvestite; he might be transgender. She was too old, she thought, to work through what all of these things meant, both to him and to her.

Regardless, she knew she'd have to find out more before she made any drive to mother's. She stayed where she was and then, after an hour, pulled into his driveway. That way she couldn't miss him when he came home. He'd know she knew his secret, whatever it was, but that was all right. Better to get the truth out, and all the truth, before the night was over.

6 After that long, harrowing, horrible day, Bernie opened the front door to a horrible surprise. A misshapen, puffy faced man with He-Man's haircut and the mustache of a TV villain stood there in a dark janitor jumpsuit. He didn't know what to make of this. No stranger ever rang his doorbell except religious nuts, and they'd never come after ten at night. That left only the police, but if this freak was the police—what kind of world would let this freak be the police?

The freak handed Bernie a Post-it note. It read:

"Do you have a cell phone in this room? If so, remove the battery now."

"It's in the bathroom," said Bernie, puzzled. He was trying to tilt his face to keep secret that fact that he had been crying.

The man snatched the Post-it out of Bernie's grasp. "Good. Let me in quickly."

"Who are you?" He was afraid, of course, that he knew the answer.

"Don't you remember me, Bernie?" the freak said in a strange, muffled voice. "I'm Theodore Anderson."

"You are not."

"I'm in disguise," the freak continued. "Let me in."

And a few moments later, the man was sitting on Bernie's couch. Bernie sat on a chair, a high-backed upholstered chair that had once, he'd been told, belonged to his grandmother, and in which he may well have never sat before. That's how confused he was.

"I thought you were coming this morning," Bernie said, breathing evenly.

"I never said that." The man leaned forwards, his elbows on his knees, and spoke quietly. "Now listen. Go to the bathroom, take the battery out of your phone. Then leave it there and come right back."

When Bernie returned, the freak was up and drawing the shades, both windows.

"I don't think the battery comes out," Bernie said.

"Then power it off and go stick it far away, whatever room is away from here. Upstairs, maybe. Your bedroom?" Bernie nodded. "Under your mattress, then. Powered off, remember."

Then the man *pulled apart*. His hair came off, and his mustache, too. Out of his mouth he pulled several wads, and as he did his cheeks sank in and his upper lip unsneered. The whole shape of his face changed. The nose, which was the worst part, peeled away with a gummy twist. In a manner of seconds, the uncanny being was revealed to be Theodore Anderson in a jumpsuit.

"Phone. Upstairs," he said. "Hurry."

Bernie obediently fetched the phone and carried it upstairs with his thumb on the power button. He could feel Anderson's eyes on him as he trudged up the steps. He was about to put the inert phone in his room, but then decided that his brother's old room, so rarely entered, just storage and half-forgotten clothes now, felt more distant. He tucked the phone behind a pile of old blankets he'd once been meaning to wash. Then he went downstairs.

Anderson was standing in the exact same place he had been when Bernie left. He was breathing perhaps a little heavier than he had been, but it slowed down quickly enough. "Listen very closely, Bernie," he said, with the woodenness of a man who has been practicing, like a telemarketer, his exact words. "Have you told anyone at all that I'll be here tonight?"

"No one, I swear!"

"Or that we had a plan, an arrangement?"

"No one!"

"Are you quite alone?"

"Yes!"

"Excellent. Will you take me on a tour of your house? I want to get the layout down in case we need it as a theater of operations."

"A theater?" Bernie asked.

"I mean, Bernard, in case we need to do things."

"Call me Bernie." And Bernie quickly showed the man around the house. It was not a large house, and yet Bernie used very little of it. His parents' old room, on the ground floor, was pretty much the same as it had been when they were alive. His brother's room upstairs with the phone.

"The phone's in here," Bernie whispered, and Anderson held a finger to his lips. He didn't say a word. He looked in every closet and even under the bed.

They went back downstairs, and into the bathroom. Anderson took a Post-it from a pocket, the one with the cell phone question, tore it to tiny pieces, and flushed them down the toilet. Several flushes followed.

Finally there was the basement. Anderson walked around the basement, which was just a grim collection of spider webs, too scary for Bernie to ever go down into. There had been snow shovels down there, and after his parents died, Bernie just bought new snow shovels. But Anderson was unconcerned.

"A fine house," he said. "Now I need you to do two things for me. First, your garbage can, your toter. Can you bring it in? Bring it into the backyard."

Bernie was mystified, but he was in no position to disobey someone who sounded like he knew what he was doing. When he rolled the toter around to the back yard, Anderson was already there. He had come out the kitchen door. He tilted the toter onto its back and pulled out two bags. Then he set the toter upright. Bernie noticed he was still wearing gloves. They went into the kitchen.

"Next," said the man, "can you check to make sure your gas tank is full, or at least half full?"

"It's pretty full," said Bernie.

"Please take your keys and go check."

"Okay, but. But what's in those bags? What was the deal with the phone?"

"Smart phones are listening devices. They listen to everything you say, and then try to sell you products. They also track your every movement."

"You're paranoid, man."

"I'm alive because I'm paranoid. I don't need to tell you what my job is. I'm paid to be paranoid."

"Fair enough, fair enough." Bernie must not have been paying attention when Anderson's precise job came up, but Bernie knew enough to play along.

"Now please go check the gas."

So Bernie did. It was three quarters, and that was fine. Everything was fine, except for the fact that Bernie didn't know what was going on.

The man didn't stop to explain, though. He just nodded and said, "I'll stay here tonight and we'll be ready for action in the morning."

Bernie wasn't sure he was allowed to ask. This man might be a ranking government agent. Possibly a colonel? But he'd been waiting so long...

"What," he said, "what are we going to do tomorrow? For action?"

Certainly Bernie had been afraid he'd get yelled at here. He was always getting yelled at. But Colin bused out an enormous smile.

"First you're going to drive while I shoot a lot of people, and then we'll turn around and I'll drive while you shoot a lot of people," he said.

"On Blande Boulevard though?"

"Yes."

"Word," said Bernie.

7 Oberman's shift had ended hours ago, but he kept his uniform on. This was somewhat against the rules, but a lot of things were somewhat against the rules. As long as it was only somewhat against the rules you could get away with it.

He dropped Campbell off and just drove around in the black and white, listening to the radio. He was aware he had staked his reputation on a disaster; he hadn't meant to, but somehow it had happened. And then nothing had happened.

Noticing the time, he called Tabitha to tell her he'd be late. He mumbled something about a work emergency.

"The massacre?" Tabitha asked. The rising inflection in her voice was hard to read. Was it excitement?

"No, no. Paperwork emergency."

When he got tired of driving through the darkening streets he pulled over into a parking lot. Then he realized it was a Dunkin' Donuts parking lot, so, just to avoid the cliché, he left and chose another parking lot. It was a bagel place, which was pretty close, but far enough away that it was not embarrassing.

The radio was silent. Oberman fished one of Campbell's cigarettes out of the crack in the seat—there was always a spare or two hidden there—and sat there looking at it. The only light was the blue neon SCHLEGEL'S BAGELS sign. Oberman looked at the blue-tinted cigarette and thought about lighting it and waited.

8 Colin had been ready, if anyone extra were at Bernie's house, to abort. He'd explain there was a big misunderstanding, use Bernie's house phone to call a cab, and get ferried back to his parked car. He had a cab company's number memorized. The bags could stay in the garbage. He'd drive home and forget the last six months had ever happened.

It would be so easy. He was already dead, and he would stay dead every day, his legs walking him around the house like a wind-up toy. "Hello, Carol. My mother's doing much better etc."

Bernie had always been the weak link in the plan. There were a thousand possible hitches, and even though Colin had made all his moves in the dark of night, some eccentric nighttime dog walker could have shone a flashlight on him. Lightning bolts or meteors could strike him down. You can't plan for everything. Colin wasn't *crazy*. But Bernie had always been the biggest risk.

And here the biggest risk, Bernard Feldstein, was playing along. The two confederates sat pleasantly in a rather squalid and congested room. There were so many boxes and items lying around, and Colin couldn't even figure out what most of them were for.

"You smoke?" Bernie asked.

"Not since high school."

"Mind if I do?"

"Knock yourself out. Just stand a little away from me please." He couldn't very well say that he didn't want his mother to smell smoke in his hair.

Bernie went to the kitchen to get some cigarettes. Colin could see clouds of cigarette smoke billowing out through the doorway. He must be puffing hard.

Colin looked around. The furniture, he noticed, was nice, or had been nice. It had "good bones" but it was stained and ratty. There were posters on the walls, but the tacks were falling out and the posters were sagging or three-cornered.

Bernie returned, cigarette expertly dangling off his lower lip. "Want something to drink?" he asked.

"We're going to stay sober. Tomorrow morning we can have coffee."

"I have lots of coffee."

"We should get a good night's sleep tonight, though. Sleepy?"

"I stay up late," Bernie said. He was looking around the room like a bad liar.

Colin knew he wasn't going to bed until Bernie was in bed. "Well, we have a lot to do first."

9 Quite some time later, Carol decided that Colin was not going to return that night. She got out of her car and walked around in the night air to stretch her legs. The sky was remarkably clear; if it were day there'd be sun, and there was never sun in April in Cottinend.

On a lark she went to Colin's door and tried it. Then she walked around to the back of the house, and tried the sliding door. To her surprise it was unlocked. Colin would never leave the house unlocked. This breach of protocol worried her more than the sex stuff, although perhaps (she admitted to herself, eventually, after she was inside and sitting on the old familiar couch) it just gave her something less scary to worry about. Something she could wrap her head around.

She slid the door open. An inexplicable pair of pliers were on the floor in front of it. The TV was blaring as she came in, and she let it play for a while. It seemed disrespectful to change the house around, not to leave it the way he left it, even if Colin would never ordinarily leave the TV on in his absence. She used the bathroom and didn't even put on the light, lest one extra light burning scare Colin off when he came home.

Then she remembered that her car was in the driveway. He'd know it was she turning lights on and off. She grabbed a remote off the coffee table and killed the TV. She considered lying down on the couch and getting some sleep. Or perhaps she could go into the bedroom and get some sleep.

Once she was in the bedroom, Carol figured that if Colin really was a transvestite he'd have to have a closet full of—she tried to think—fishnets? or bustiers?

She started looking for them.

10

Seamus Donofrio left his house with his wife's damned dog that always wanted to go for a walk when Seamus wanted to sleep. Let it go in the back yard, Seamus figured, but his wife was afraid the dog would soil her garden. Her "prize petunias," Seamus called them, although he didn't know if there were actually petunias there. He didn't know what petunias looked like.

Anyway (he explained to the officer on the phone, later), Seamus was walking his wife's dog, which should have been her responsibility, except she said she didn't feel safe at night. Imagine not feeling safe in Cottinend! Why should Seamus feel safe, then? But Rano was a busy street, and there were plenty of street lights, and porch lights. Maybe bring a flashlight! Even if people weren't walking around, if you yelled, someone would hear you. All you'd have to do was yell.

The damned dog was sniffing everything, doing everything except, you know, its business. It sniffed at a car parked on the side of the road and only after standing there in the horrible stink of the exhaust did Seamus realize the car was idling.

"Don't piss there!" Seamus told the dog, with a jerk on the leash. "They'll be right back." All Seamus needed was some meathead to come out and catch this dog soiling his ancient wreck of a car. He could blame Seamus for all the dents and rust stains. Was that a broken window? He could blame Seamus for that too. He dragged the unwilling dog along, dragged it while it stiff-legged dug in its heels. It was like moving a table across the kitchen floor.

Don't get Seamus started on how many times he'd had to move the kitchen table!

After what seemed like forever—an hour maybe?—the dog completed its business, you know, and Seamus ambled back home. He walked along Rano, and there was that same car, still idling.

When he got home, as his wife was screeching, "What happened, Seamus? Seamus, what's wrong? What is it? Seamus? Seamus, what happened?" he called the police from the kitchen phone.

11 Colin was aware that Bernie had spent the last twenty minutes nervously pretending to putter around the house, performing simple tasks. He picked up and set down small items, mostly garbage. Looking busy.

But once Colin took the rifle out of the bag, there was no more pretense. Bernie just stared and smoked and smoked and stared as Colin looked the weapon over to make sure nothing had obviously broken from its drop into the trash can. A little pacing, maybe; mostly staring.

"You're what? Going to clean and oil it?" Bernie asked eagerly. "Take it all apart and check each piece? Then screw it back together? Like a Q?"

"A Q?"

Bernie mimed playing pool. "A cue."

The thing was, Colin had no idea how to clean or oil a rifle. Taking the time to learn a single thing about maintenance would have ruined his reputation as someone completely uninterested in guns.

"No oil needed," he said. "This model is self-lubricating."

He could have sworn that Bernie choked back a laugh.

12 Theodore Anderson was now unzipping a ratty old duffel bag. He took out two grotesque masks covered in freckles and tossed one to Bernie. "Try this on."

The mask looked in bad shape. It smelled stale, like a basement. Bernie spent a moment looking at it. It almost looked familiar.

"Don't worry," Col. Anderson said, "no one will know you were involved."

Bernie almost jumped up, but of course he was already standing. "No one will know?"

The Colonel stopped rummaging through the bag. "You want someone to know?"

And that was a new one on Bernie. He had always half assumed that he would be famous afterwards, that he'd walk into work and get those high fives all around. He knew that didn't actually make sense, when he thought about it. He knew that no one would be happy that he killed people. It was the Alan situation all over again. But if this whole exercise wasn't going to change his status, what was the point of it?

Ah, but he'd answered his own question. There was one point. The smirking, wicked face of Alan Jancewicz.

"I'm in," said Bernie.

"I know you're in," said Col. Anderson. "I was asking if you want to get caught."

"Oh. No."

"Good. We'll take every precaution. You have nothing to worry about."

"Your gun is untraceable. Your car in untraceable." Bernie said it as a matter of course. He knew how these things worked. He wanted to show that he was not a complete fool.

"We're taking your car, actually."

"What? No way!"

"Don't worry, we'll be covering up the license plate. Like you say, untraceable. It's unlikely they'll be any witnesses, anyway. Just in case, try on the mask."

Anderson had brought out of the duffel bag four pieces of plastic. They looked like bookends from the future. They looked like crab's claws. Then he brought out a great many ammo magazines and several boxes of long, cool bullets. One by one he started inserting the bullets into the magazine. Each one snapped home with a satisfying click. To Bernie it looked like nothing so much as loading up a Pez dispenser. But it was more exciting than a Pez dispenser. Bernie felt the way he always felt at a strip club. He just wanted to touch something.

So there was this one time Col. Anderson got up to take a piss. Bernie immediately picked up the rifle. He tried sighting it, sniper style. He then picked up a magazine. It was comically long. He fumbled it into place, and it hung low like a waddle from the underside of the rifle. "This is its dick," Bernie said to an imaginary audience.

He raised the rifle to his shoulder again and looked down its barrel. It had no scope, which probably just showed what a skilled sniper the Colonel was. He looked for a target outside, but of course all the shades had been drawn. Finally he decided to point it at the TV, because the TV would probably explode when he shot it.

Nothing happened, though, when he pulled the trigger.

Suddenly something rough was yanking the rifle from his grip, His finger caught painfully and twisted. Some skin came off. There beside him, rifle in hand, stood Col. Theodore Anderson, and the man looked furious. Usually when Bernie saw a face like that he was about to get fired. This time, he thought, he might actually get shot.

To save his life, Bernie tried to be helpful. "The gun's broken," he said.

Anderson took some deep breaths. "The trigger reads your prints. I didn't authorize yours yet, and fortunately, too. If you'd shot that in here you would have ruined the whole mission."

"Sorry. Sorry, sorry."

"We have to be extremely careful with the rifle. It has a hair trigger if your prints are authorized. Why do you think I wear gloves?"

13 Well after midnight, Oberman abandoned his watch. The tenth was over, and there had been nothing more interesting on the police band than an abandoned car.

Time to drive home and go to sleep. He had always needed at least eight hours to function properly, so it was already too late for him. He had to be in at seven o'clock tomorrow; where everyone would spend the day making fun of him.

He knew he should be grateful that April tenth was a dud, and on a conscious level he was. But you must understand that he had also wanted to be right.

14 Many of the carefully enumerated contents of the duffel bag were now scattered around Bernie's living room floor. Colin was filling magazine after magazine with bullets. Fortunately this was extremely easy to do. It might have been tedious if he had not been giving such attention to each bullet, lest any go in crooked or askew. One of the magazines, the one with a black Sharpied X on it, was the magazine he'd been practicing with all these months; he'd been practicing with several of them, of course, but this was the one he'd been practicing with *full*, to make sure the weight was right, and he didn't know if rattling around full all those months may have caused some kind of internal damage. Maybe it would jam. He removed all the bullets, one by one, and then reinserted five—only five—of them.

Worst of all, he had to urinate. He'd left the bathroom door open a crack before, and he'd seen Bernie fussing with the rifle before he'd actually gotten to relieve himself. Only the safety had saved everything. Of course, Colin could pick up the rifle and carry it to the bathroom, but who knew what mischief Bernie might get into with the magazines? He couldn't carry *everything* into the bathroom. It would be easier to carry Bernie. He'd just have to hold it in.

But then he also needed to get rid of Bernie for the next part of the plan. "I'm going to cover up your license plate, but I need your help," he said, after a few moments' thought. "Can you turn the car around, you know, back it into the driveway? Push the passenger seat as far back as it can go. Then turn off the engine and the lights, but wait in the car keeping lookout until I knock on the window. Then we'll go inside the house one at a time, me first. Leave the car unlocked. Got it?"

Bernie said he did.

"Can you repeat the steps?"

He more or less could.

Bernie went out alone and started the car. After a minute the engine cut, and Colin went out with the cardboard, the blackened cardboard with the thread taped on. That car had to have been much older than Bernie, perhaps older than Colin. It was not in good shape. There was a bumper sticker for D.A.R.E that had obviously once read DARE TO KEEP KIDS OFF DRUGS but had been doctored with an x-acto to read DARE TO KEEP DRUGS. Crouching in the dark behind the rusted trunk, Colin freed one end of the black thread. He hooked the creased end of the cardboard over the license plate. Then he unwound the thread, passed it behind the right rear wheel, catching it on a tread, and wrapped it around one of the nuts. Tap on the window and head inside. From the door, slightly open, he watched Bernie exit the car. He watched as Bernie's head turned, in the dark driveway, towards the black space where the license plate had been. And there Bernie nodded appreciatively.

Colin had practiced this is his own garage, rolling his car back and forth three feet, and he knew that as soon as the wheel started to turn it would whip the cardboard off the plate. The whole thing was a dodge, a spoof for Bernie's benefit. Only an idiot would go out driving with an obscured plate—the first cop they passed would've stopped them. With the car turned around, no neighbor would even see the plate. The cover could stay on all night long.

He was rather proud of this trick. He'd remembered what Bernie had told him, the Pennsylvania plates. Unlike New York, Pennsylvania does not require front license plates. Perhaps it was unnecessary, but if it kept Bernie from complaining about using his car, all the better. If they couldn't use Bernie's car—well, with the Ridgemont Rest car doubtless gone by this point, they'd have to kill one of Bernie's neighbors and take his car, and that extra complication, although hardly impossible, sounded unpleasant. Surely it was hard enough living next to Bernie Feldstein without having to die for it.

The spool of thread, the Sharpie: needless to say he'd thrown them both out weeks ago, shortly after preparing the Post-its.

Bernie came back in, and Colin ate one sandwich and a banana. Bernie ate pretzels and watched him.

"Where's your garbage?" Colin asked, banana peel in hand.

"Oh, I threw it out back."

"I mean, your garbage can. Your inside garbage can for throwing trash in. I didn't see one in the kitchen before."

"Yeah, I don't have a garbage can inside. I just carry stuff out to the toter."

Colin put the peel into one of the trash bags he'd brought. He sat down on the floor again, cross-legged, the rifle at his side and half under his knee. He started setting up the tape holders, jamming seven full magazines into each.

"That's also like Pez," Bernie said as he watched the spring-loaded action.

"I don't know what that means," said Colin.

15

All the work was done, and Bernie could tell that the Colonel was hinting they should go to bed. But Bernie had slept most of the day; and anyway he was too excited to sleep; and anyway he was terrified of the morning, which would, as he understood it, come sooner if he slept. But the Colonel just sat there on the couch, his knees together, in what was probably a military pose. Bernie was in danger of getting bored.

"Can't I go get my phone?" he asked.

"You can't use your phone until the mission is over," Col. Anderson said, "but in a little while you can go get it."

"Oh, okay. I thought there might be news we could use on it."

"News?"

"Spies and things like that."

"Your phone will betray you. When you need it most, it will let you down," Col. Anderson said. "I never take a phone into a tactical situation."

"Do you want to play Xbox?"

"You should simply go to bed."

"I don't think I can sleep," Bernie said, lighting up another cigarette. This was the most he'd smoked in a non-pizza environment in years. It was just that he knew what he was doing when lighting up, or ashing, or even in blowing the smoke out his nose. Anything else he tried to do there was a pretty good chance he would bungle. He had to keep smoking to conceal his incompetence.

"Fine. Do you have cards?" the Colonel asked.

"Sure."

"A pinochle deck?"

"What?"

"Just get the cards, I guess. I'm going to get a glass of water. Glasses in the cupboard?"

Bernie had probably not drunk straight water for three solid years, but he said, "Get me one, too," just to fit in, and then in a panic followed it with "please" and then "sir."

As the Colonel went to the kitchen, Bernie started bumping through some drawers in his parents' old room. He finally found a pack held together with a rubber band so old it splintered like wood and fell in half when he touched it. A dark stain marked the back of the cards where the band had been.

He came back to the living room as the Colonel entered, two coffee mugs in his hands.

"I couldn't find glasses," he said half apologetically, holding one out. It sounded odd coming from him, but he was probably just being polite. Bernie took the proffered mug, and then noticed the one the Colonel was going to drink from. He hadn't seen it it years. It said WORLD'S GREATEST MOM #1 over a picture of a koala.

"Not that one, not that one," said Bernie, and he stepped forward and took it right from the Colonel's hand. He had acted without thinking, but he suddenly remembered that Theodore Anderson was a trained combat veteran and could kill him with his bare hands. He froze, wondering if he was going to die.

But the Colonel just took the other mug from Bernie. It simply said FELDSTEIN and sported an etymology. *Field + stone*, essentially, although the mug spelled it out with more words. Bernie didn't give a rat's ass about that mug; he didn't even remember ever having seen it before.

He could see the Colonel shaking his head and smiling. The Colonel sipped some water as he walked away.

Bernie took the koala mug back into the kitchen, and dumped the water out in the sink so he wouldn't have to pretend to drink it. When was the last time he'd seen that koala? Fifteen years? He noticed a partially open cupboard, and realized he had probably never looked inside it, at least not since his childhood. When he opened it further, he saw it was filled with mugs. He carefully put the koala mug back in the cupboard. He didn't want to get in a car and shoot anybody right now, he just wanted to look through the old mugs. Some of them looked familiar, or at least triggered a weird ghost of a memory, like a dream from two nights before.

He wanted a reprieve. He wanted to shoot Alan Jancewicz not later today but tomorrow.

And as he came back to the living room he was about to ask for a day's delay. The Colonel, who was sitting with his mug on the couch, spoke first, though.

"Did you grow up here?" he asked.

"Yeah. It was my parents' house."

"Your parents...?"

"Both dead. Cancer. They smoked."

"You smoke," said the Colonel.

"Who wants to live forever?"

"Who wants to die from cancer of all things?" said the Colonel; but he left it at that.

"It's cool having my own house," Bernie went on. He was aiming to impress. He was talking like a first date. "It's paid off. Not by me, you know. But it's paid off, and that makes things easier."

"Sure," said the Colonel. "Gives you one up on the other fellers."

"I've never been one up on anyone," Bernie snapped.

"Not everyone owns a house," said the Colonel. He was so blasé about it, so *cool*, that it was making Bernie furious.

"What? Do you own a house?"

"That's classified."

"Come on, no one can guess your secret identity from one stupid fact. Do you own a house, yes or no?"

The Colonel looked amused by this outburst. He took a sip of water. Then he said, "Okay, yes. I own at least one house."

"And college? Do you have to go to college to join the FBI?"

"You actually have to go through law school to join the FBI."

"I never got to go to college! I never got to do anything!"

"You're what? In your twenties? You could still go to college now."

"I can't afford college!" He could hear—and it embarrassed him—his voice breaking, but he remembered with shame that he did once, in fact, against the advice of his guidance counselor and parents, start to apply to college. He'd called a toll-free number himself, secretly, to get the application. Oh, he'd had dreams of life on the beach, coeds in bikinis, summer all year long—his idea of college had been shaped by movies, and more specifically certain kinds of movies. Only after he'd filled out the forms and asked for reluctant recommendations and painstakingly written an essay on his greatest achievement, which probably should not have relied, in retrospect, as heavily on video games as it did —only after all of that, as he was addressing the envelope, did he perceive and realize that Miami University was in Ohio.

"You probably meant University of Miami," said Sarah, who might have become his girlfriend except Bernie, anticipating all the Miami tail, had told her he didn't want to commit to any local girls.

"You never would have gotten into either one, dude," Stone said. And that was true. But it was too close to deadline for a University of Miami application to get ready, so he'd never know for certain.

The Colonel, meanwhile, despite the pity and rage on Bernie's face, was speaking calmly. "You could join the army. Get a GI Bill type thing."

Bernie snorted. "You think I didn't try to join the army? If they'd let me in the army, everything would have been different. If they'd let me go to college everything would have been different. My brother got to go to college! But I made one stupid mistake when I was a kid, I beat up the wrong guy—"

"You told me a slightly different story last time," the Colonel said, "when you were drunker. The shit lottery?"

Bernie pressed on, "What if I'd been like you? I'd be a secret agent, not some loser lying to his boss to get one lousy day off. I'd be doing great things if I went college like you."

The face Col. Theodore Anderson was now sporting was hard to read. He looked like he was thinking.

"I wouldn't be some asshole at a pizza place!" Bernie went on, practically jumping up and down. "I would't be up all night so I could do something stupid for some CIA sting! Wait…are you CIA or FBI?"

"That's classified," the Colonel said, but he seemed to say it automatically, while his mind was a thousand miles away.

"Classified? Fuck you, classified! I'm going to go shoot people I think I deserve to know—"

And then Bernie stopped abruptly. He was worried he'd gone too far. Even if the Colonel were not combat certified, he had three inches and fifty pounds on Bernie and he owned a gun. And the queer look on his face…was that the face you made before you killed someone? Stone had told Bernie just the other day that once in a bar fight a marine had picked up another guy and just crushed him into a ball, breaking all his bones. Then the marine just rolled him away, like a giant bean bag. He said there was a video of the kill, but YouTube had removed it. Bernie didn't want to die that way. He was standing and the Colonel was sitting, but he still felt naked and towered over.

But after a moment, the Colonel said, "I have four things to tell you." He had something like a smile in his eyes, but that was scarier than anything else.

"You mean four things before I die?" asked Bernie pathetically.

"Four things. First, keep your voice down when you're on a mission. Technically you're in the field right now, even though it's your own house. That's one.

"Second: Classified is classified and no amount of whining about who deserves what is going to change your clearance. That's two.

"Third: You don't know all that. You don't know where you'd end up. Every moment of your life could have gone right and tomorrow might still be your finest hour. You could be a Rhodes scholar and a champion—what sport do you like?"

"Wrestling."

"—a champion wrestler, and it might not matter. You can still end up an asshole at a pizza parlor."

"Ring of Honor, not WWE."

"It doesn't matter. You might have your back against the wall when you find yourself here tonight. There's no way around it. Anyone could find himself at the Incident. You can't know where you'll end up. All you can do is see through your own bullshit. That's three.

"And fourth: You don't have to do this, you know. You're a volunteer. You can back out. All you have to do is say the word, and I leave. You take an oath not to tell anyone anything ever, and I go away, like none of this ever happened."

"What? You're not going to kill me?"

"You're not on the list. But you do have to choose now. By tomorrow morning, you'll be locked in. So what is it going to be? Are you in or are you out?"

Bernie usually knew what do in a situation like this. Well, he'd never been in a situation *like this*, but whenever people asked Bernie a question, he just figured out, from tone of voice or facial expression, what answer they wanted. If he'd learned the trick earlier, he might have done better in school; but at least it had let him graduate.

The Colonel's expression, though, was a blank. His tone was dry and level. He seemed to have no opinion on which way Bernie would choose. Bernie looked in the Colonel's eyes, and at first he merely thought they were deep, but as he looked more he saw that deep was the wrong word. They simply had no bottom. There was nothing to see because the viewer looked through and out the other side.

To be perfectly honest, Bernie was not really in the habit of thinking. But: Had he not gotten smarter? Had he not outfoxed the spies and hackers? Had he not concealed from Stone and Randall the impending glory?

The sun rose and the sun set as Bernie stood in thought. But it was just a car, its headlights momentary sliding under the blinds. If Bernie backed down now, what was there to do tomorrow? Pizza and smokes? Amber, maybe? Would Amber date a man who had never killed another man? *Probably,* but what if that man were Bernie? *No,* right? Was she even a spy?

"Just say yes or no," the Colonel said.

But Bernie did not say yes or no. He was just thinking: Pizza and smokes, and Prishtine and Call of Duty, and nothing else, day after day forever.

"You have to choose," the Colonel said.

But Bernie did not choose. He stood there, no longer thinking but perhaps looking like he was thinking. All of his effort was spent sending a psychic message to the Colonel, who had perhaps been trained in psychic warfare reception. "Choose," was the message he sent. "Choose for me."

And he did. "Just tell me if you're backing out," the Colonel said. "If you say nothing I'll assume you're committed." And after a moment Colonel Theodore Anderson nodded—he was always nodding, except when he was shaking his head. He seemed to be constantly baffled and incredulous, except he also seemed very certain and authoritative. "That's that, then. You're in, and there's no backing out. Then you'll have to go to bed, now, and no excuses."

"I found cards, though."

"Hmmm. Count them."

The deck had forty-eight cards, which apparently would have been all right, the Colonel said, for a pinochle deck, whatever that was. But it was no good for this one. It was no good for stalling.

The Colonel set his cup on the floor. He stood up. "Go get your phone, the one under your mattress. Don't turn it on—I'll know if you turn it on. Put it in a sock and bring it to me. After that: bed, and you can count sheep if you need to."

He had stood up. It was clear, from his face, what he wanted. So what else was there for Bernie to do?

16 Seamus had told the whole story to Officer Boothe while Officer Cechlovsky walked down the street to check out the car. After a few minutes, Boothe joined her.

"No key in the ignition," Cechlovsky said.

"How're we supposed to turn it off then? Should we call a tow truck?"

"If we're going to take it someplace, one of us can just drive it, you know."

Boothe shook his head. "Mess up the evidence."

"What evidence? Is there even a crime being committed here?"

"Well, we can't just leave it here, can we?"

Cechlovsky considered. "You know what I wish? If that idiot Oberman was on duty, he could do that thing he does, where he takes the spark plugs out or something."

"Beats me," said Boothe. "I don't know jack about cars."

They called a tow truck.

17 Bernie, for the life of him, could not find the phone. It wasn't under his mattress. It wasn't anywhere in his room. He finally found an old bar of soap in the back of a closet. He slipped it into a sock, hoping against hope that the Colonel would not use it to beat him to death.

18 Carol had discovered that the mystery drawer she'd snooped through back in January was empty. She had discovered nothing else. If there was pornography hidden in the house it was neither under the mattress or behind the drawers, and nothing would answer her questions as much as Colin's pornography preferences.

She picked up a Post-it pad from the kitchen and held it, slantwise, to the light, to see if there were any indentations. Maybe she could see what had been written on the sheet above, catch a clue…

But the sheet was smooth. It might as well have been part of a brand-new pack. It was like the rest of Colin's house: There was nothing there.

Had there ever been a home so bereft of any scandal? Even the basement—mysteriously left unlocked tonight—where she'd honestly expected to find some sort of man-cave or possibly sex-dungeon—was implausibly clean.

She came back to the kitchen, and there she had her first surprise. Colin's phone, which he would never leave the house without, was sitting on the counter, charging. Or charged. She'd walked past it a dozen times searching for clues, but of course it didn't *look* odd or out of place. Only the fact that it was here and Colin was not.

With his phone in her hand, she sat down on the living room couch. Perhaps an old email or a text conversation could give her some insights. She kicked off her shoes and lay down against the soft pillows, but the results were disappointing. The only non-work-related texts were from her. There was nothing unusual—there was *nothing else at all*—on the phone, except for a missed call—a New York number—and a new voice mail. New and unheard.

And here Carol paused. She could listen to the voice mail, but she had no idea, afterwards, how to conceal the fact that she had listened to the voice mail. She'd have to delete it, and then, if the person called back—Colin would know she'd invaded his privacy. It seemed like an extra, fatal step too far. She set the phone down on the ground, and closed her eyes, hoping to get some rest before Colin returned.

But the couch was uncomfortable, the soft pillows too soft, and after a while she went upstairs for one last night in Colin's bed.

She tossed about and couldn't sleep, and when she finally decided to listen to the damned voice mail, she realized she'd left the phone all the way downstairs, and screw it.

19 Colin accepted the proffered sock. "What took you so long?" he asked. ¶ "I couldn't find a sock with no holes in it," said that nervous idiot. ¶ Colin waited for Bernie to go back upstairs to sleep. He took the sock to the basement door and threw it down to the bottom of the stairs, hearing a thump. Whether such a drop would break a phone or not—it didn't really matter. He closed the door.

He'd held it in while Bernie was awake, but now he went to the bathroom to micturate. He unzipped and was about to go when he realized he might spatter. Was there DNA in urine? He sat on the toilet. Afterwards he wiped the seat down with sterile wipes. Then, to be certain, the floor.

He got cushions from the couch and made a makeshift bed at the foot of the stairs. For blankets he used coats from the coat closet. He set the timer on the stove as an alarm clock and lay down and closed his eyes and went right to sleep.

20 School shootings are just a special case of rampage killings, and there are plenty of other, more common rampage killings: workplace shootings, especially. Postal workers snap and open fire at the office pretty often, don't they? Lots of people do it. Students do it, too.

But everyone has noticed that school shootings tend to be deadlier than other kinds of rampages. Columbine (1999)—15 dead; Virginia Tech (2007)—33 dead;

Parkland (2018)—17 dead. Even Charles Whitman, the ur-rampager—13 dead in 1966—was an architecture student at U. of Texas Austin. Most postal workers are lucky if they can kill two or three coworkers before the cops take them out.

Sociologists and aficionados developed a theory for why student murderers tended to be deadlier than office workers. The theory was that most workers, before they kill, get mad, go home, get a gun, go back to work, and open fire. They planned for three minutes, tops. Because if any grown-up human spent more than three minutes thinking about the rampage, he'd stop. He wouldn't do it. Once those few minutes of blinding rage go away, you're not going to kill anyone. Your reality principle reasserts itself.

But a teenager, or even a college student, can think about murder for months or years. He just keeps working on the plan. Seung-Hui Cho brought chains and chained the doors of his university building shut. Postal Workers wouldn't think to do that.

The theory started to unravel after Newtown, Connecticut—27 killed at Sandy Hook Elementary by a man who was not a student—but at least the killer was only twenty years old. But then well-planned, exceptionally deadly mass shootings started cropping up perpetrated by actual grown-ups with jobs and everything. The First Baptist Church in Sutherland Springs, Texas. The Pulse nightclub in Orlando. Route 91 Harvest festival on the Las Vegas strip.

It turned out, revised theories held, that the key to a deadly shooting had less to do with the age of the perpetrator than with the location of the shooting. School shootings were deadly only because schools are particularly ripe with possibility for murder: the concentration of population and their captive nature: Primary and secondary students are forbidden by law to leave the building. Any place that's hard to escape from will do as well.

It was all, as the realtors say, location etc. And perhaps that night in their dreams Colin and Bernie both pre-visited that location their luck or destiny had lighted on.

Tomorrow they would drive along Blande Boulevard.

In those dreadful days, five wicked priests' heads shall be sold for a penny,
Slaughter shall rage to such a degree,
  And infants left by those that are slain
That damsels shall with fear and glee
  Cry, "Mother, mother, here's a man !"
  • *The Original Predictions of Robert Nixon* (1798?).

v. One Long Morning.

Carol Wernick • Colin Lang • John Oberman • Ronnie • Bernie Feldstein • John Oberman • Amber Meir • Colin Lang • John Oberman • Cottinend, N.Y. • The Sp!der • Bernie Feldstein • Sergeant Gaye • Colin Lang • John Oberman • Bernie Feldstein • Colin Lang • Bernie Feldstein • Colin Lang • Alan Jancewicz • John Oberman • Alan Jancewicz • John Oberman • Colin Lang • John Oberman • Carol Wernick's voice mail • Colin Lang • Sergeant Gaye • John Oberman • Alan Jancewicz • Colin Lang • Carol Wernick

1 Some time around dawn, wrapped in Colin's comforter on his 600-count Egyptian cotton sheets, Carol drifted into a slumber at first fretful and filled with nervous dreams and later dead deep and dreamless.

2 The buzzer on the stove went off after he was already up and making instant coffee. There'd been little chance he'd oversleep, but it was good to have a failsafe. He shut it off.

In many ways this morning was no different from any other morning. He ran the plan over in his head, focusing on exact steps he would have to take in the exact order. Here he was in a strange kitchen, drinking from a mug that advertised a radio station he'd never listened to, but it felt like he had been here a hundred times before—not *exactly* here, because the concrete details were new, but essentially here. He'd assumed Bernie would have coffee, and that he'd get a chance to drink some, even if he hadn't known what the mug would look like.

He looked around at the concrete details. Bernie probably should have cleaned up his kitchen.

It had been so long since Colin had removed his gloves; he could feel his fingers starting to wrinkle, like a bather's. He went to the bathroom, turned on both taps, took off the gloves, and washed his hands with soap. When he was done he turned off the taps with the side of a wrist. Returning to the kitchen, he washed the coffee mug carefully, then soaped it up and left it sitting in dishwater. He walked around barehanded, holding his hands up like a woman drying her nails.

For the scorekeepers: Colin ate the second cheese sandwich. Fingerprints on the sandwich, but of course the evidence was in his belly. Then he put his gloves back on. Just for good measure he gave everything, including the cylinder of sterile wipes, a good sterile wipe down. He wiped the gloves down, too, because he had not brought the pliers. He flushed the wipes and set the cylinder under the sink, as though it belonged there.

After a while, the man himself, Bernie, came staggering into the kitchen with his hair wild. "What time is it?" he cried in a panic.

Colin tried to determine if Bernie was still asleep, suffering from a night terror of some sort. "We have plenty of time," he said. "It's a little after seven thirty."

Bernie sank into a chair. The plastic cushion made a little burping sigh as he put his weight on it.

"It might help," Colin added, "if you just do your morning routine. Do you usually brush your teeth in the morning?"

Bernie looked up suddenly, like a man just caught sleeping on the job, or perusing pornography. "Yes. Yes, always. Usually. Just not today."

"Okay," said Colin. "Have some coffee." He reached into the cupboard and took down a mug at random. It had a crayon drawing and the words THANK YOU FOR BEING A DAD. Colin put it back and chose another one, one with two Transformers robots humping each other. "Okay, I'm going to pack up," he said. "We have a couple more things to do here, but we have to be ready to hit the road at five after nine."

"Wait, what? No!" The *no* was a toddler's *no*, bright with fury. It was the first *no* of a tantrum, before anyone was purple; but purple was coming. It was not a *no* Colin wanted to hear.

"Bernie," he said, stern but kindly, "the whole mission has been planned out. There's a timetable."

"No way. We'll get to Blande by like nine fifteen! I'm not doing it! I'm not going!"

Colin had little experience dealing with tantrums. "Why? Why do you even care?"

"The road's not long enough! I'm not going!"

"You're not making any sense. Please explain. When do you want to go?"

"An hour later. Ten fifteen."

"We can't do it an hour la—"

"You have to do it one hour later or I'm out!"

"You can't—"

"I'm out! I'm out! I'm out!"

"Stop! Shut up, just let me think." Colin turned away. Clearly Bernie had some agenda of his own. Colin had taken Bernie's Blande Boulevard idea as a simple stroke of genius. From the mouths of babes, as they say. But there was something else behind it, and even during the pointless hours of the night, Colin had never bothered to find out what it was. This was an oversight.

But there was no point grieving over the past. The question was how to salvage the situation.

Everything had been planned to get Colin to Sunset Grove at the normal time. In fact, the "normal time" had been selected to get him to the Incident during optimal traffic. To change the time now—an hour later's start meant he'd be an hour late for mother. He shouldn't be an hour late because today of all days he couldn't behave abnormally. Abnormal was suspicious.

Could he get to Sunset Grove quicker? He could avoid going home, he could drive there straight from Route 434 afterwards. He had, as he always had, that change of clothes in the trunk, under the garbage bags; he'd be overdressed but he could leave off the tie. It would mean he wouldn't have his phone, though, which would itself be abnormal. But people did forget their phones. That was a thing that could happen. But that would save him fifteen, twenty minutes tops. He'd still be late.

What if he had a reason for being late? What if he tried to take Blande to get to I-81? There would certainly be a traffic jam in the aftermath. Just get caught in the traffic jam; since he forgot his phone he couldn't even call ahead to explain.

Of course, driving from his car from Route 434 all the way around to Blande would eat up the fifteen minutes he'd save by not going home. But that hardly mattered, since with the excuse of a traffic jam he could be as late as he wanted. As a cover story it wasn't flawless, but it would only fall apart if the news reports were precise about the start time of the incident *and* people were certain about how long it took to get to Sunset Grove from one obscure street in Cottinend. If someone had to do math to catch you out in a lie, you were probably safe. Especially if the would-be mathematicians were the patrons and staff of Sunset Grove.

"Okay," he said. "Okay, we go an hour later. But that, listen to me, that is the only change. You do what I say after this."

"Of course, of course. Yes, thank you, thank you."

Colin sat down. He stuck his feet out like a cartoon dad at the end of the day.

"Can I smoke? I need a smoke," Bernie said. Colin only nodded. "You want one?"

"Nah." Mother, and all. "Finish your cigarette," Colin said. "Then get dressed and let's get you into uniform. Then we talk about what's the big deal with the time change."

But Colin was busy running the new plan over and over in his head. He honestly had trouble remembering things he had never erased from the white board. He was wishing he'd saved the banana. Was there any other loose ends that the time change left? Colin ran through the possibilities one by one until he got to Carol.

It was always Carol.

Colin went back to his duffel bag, where phone and the battery still lay together in their plastic bag. He popped the battery in and powered up the phone.

"I'm going to call headquarters," Colin called to Bernie as he headed for the stairs.

"But you said no phones when—"

"You're the one who changed the time. There are consequences." He walked up the stairs as he dialed, from memory, Carol's number. It would never do to have her calling his mother before he arrived; his mother panicking over simple tardiness was enough to deal with; he didn't need Carol panicking as well.

At the top of the stairs he went over the lie in his head until it sounded plausible.

"Hey, honey. This is Colin. So good to hear your voice, even in a recording. I'm actually calling from Sunset Grove, that's why you don't recognize the number. I got here early. My mother, they're actually trying her in a room in the memory ward. They don't let you use cell phones because of all the pacemakers and whatever these beeping machines are. So don't call me here; I'll give you a ring as soon as I can with more information." More tenderly: "I hope to see you soon."

As soon as he hung up, Colin realized he'd left Bernie downstairs unsupervised with the rifle. He hurried down. The phone was in his pocket. Nobody ever did talk about the time change and Alan Jancewicz.

3 Officer Oberman slept through his alarm, but his girlfriend rolled him out of bed. He was running late. He stumbled through a shower and a perfunctory shave. He drove to pick up Campbell.

"I see you managed to defuse that bomb, eh?" Campbell said.

"Har har."

"Get used to it. You're going to hear that about a million times today."

By the end of roll call he'd heard it fifteen.

4 The phone by the bed rang at 6:30, and caller ID said it was Mickey's cell phone. Ronnie shoved her husband until he woke up and agreed to answer it. Ronnie had put off calling her cousin back all yesterday, and had hoped she could put it off for another day or two, but this constant hounding was wearing her down. She'd have to give him the name, *Bernard Feldstein*, sometime today.

She just hoped it was the right Nardo. She didn't know what she'd say if she was supposed to call the pizza place back.

Nevertheless, if she had to talk to Mickey today, she was not going to do it at 6:30 in the morning, and she certainly was not going to do it from home. At work there was the opportunity to be busy and get off the phone fast.

She could hear the conversation, Mickey's frantic, overloud begging for her, her husband's groggy and implausible excuse that she was already at work.

"Well, where does she work?" she heard her cousin shout.

"I can't believe you don't know what your own cousin does," Liam said.

"I know what she *does*, of course, obviously," Mickey's voice bellowed through the phone, "I just don't know the number."

"She's not supposed to take calls at work," Liam told him and hung up. "Jesus, Ronnie," he said, "are you sure this is your cousin? He acts like a desperate ex."

"I don't even understand why I had to lie and get this Nardo guy's name in the first place," she said, "I'm half tempted to just tell him his name is Smith."

5 The jumpsuit Agent Anderson was wearing, and which he wanted Bernie to put on now, was not cool. It was black, which was fine, but it was also canvas or something. Two zippers ran from the shoulders all the way down along the legs. To put it on you had to slide your arms through the sleeves, pull the dangling loincloth part around in front of you and attach it with a zipper at the legs. This was the whole inseam and the "bib" part of the top. You zipped both zippers up while holding the bib with your chin, connecting the inner leg and the outer leg and then going up to your shoulders. It was ridiculously hard, and once Bernie had (after much negotiation, instruction, false starts, failures) done it he had no idea how he was going to go to the bathroom.

The whole point (Anderson explained) was that you could strip the jumpsuit off without removing your shoes. If they took as long to remove as they did to put on then you might as well just take your shoes off! But Anderson pointed out that Bernie might end up standing on broken glass, or an electrified floor and would need to keep his shoes on. Bernie dug out his winter boots from the back of the closet so at least he would have something large to unzip them around.

The Colonel was packing things into a trash bag: the windbreaker, the plastic squeezers with magazines in them. Extra boxes of ammo went in too. From another trash bag; he extracted the nose putty and cotton from the night before; then he tossed in a banana peel and a grocery circular.

Two magazines remained out, and he selected one, one with a black X on it. He loaded it in the rifle.

"Are you almost ready?" he asked.

"Yeah, I'm ready." The coveralls were far too large on Bernie, but it didn't seem the time to mention it.

"Any last trips to the bathroom? Anything at all?"

"Um. What should I bring?"

"Keys. Your mask. That's it."

"Wallet?" Bernie asked.

"It doesn't matter. If a cop wants to pull you over, follow my lead, and we'll either shoot him or drive like hell."

"Follow your lead?"

"Do what I say."

"I knew that."

Bernie was having a hard time believing all of this was real. It had been, for so long, a fantasy. It was easier to imagine that it was still a fantasy, that every part of this was an elaborate game. He only wished it was more fun.

"Because when you're ready, I need you to practice shooting."

Bingo! Bernie had shot paintball guns, and once, when he was about thirteen, Stone's stepfather's borrowed pistol at some squirrels. This rifle was so much larger and deadlier!

"Did you register my prints?"

But of course he did!

"As soon as you're done with the magazine, we're going to leave, walk quickly to the car. In fact, you go out and open the car's two front doors right now and leave them open."

"It's a two door."

"Right. Both doors, then."

Bernie did this. "I can shoot it now?" he said as he reentered the house. Anderson had taken the moment to put his wig back on. He was trying to straighten out the nose putty.

"Hang on. After you shoot, we're going to hurry to the car. Don't lock the house, in case we need to come back in. Start the car up and drive away quickly. Peel out, and don't slow down till you're off this street. Follow my directions to Blande—"

"I know the way—"

"We have something to do on the way. Follow my directions to Blande Boulevard. I'll be hunkered down in the car so it only looks like there's one person in it. That's you. It gives us the element of surprise."

"Makes sense." Bernie was trying to act cool. He even had an unlit cigarette in his mouth.

"Drive exactly five miles over the speed limit the whole way. Once we get to Blande you can drive fast if there are no cars in front of us, but slow down if you see one. We don't want to get close to anyone in the front. It's best if we never see anyone in front of us, but it would be nice if we didn't see anyone behind us, either. If you can pace it that way. That'd be just luck, but the most important thing is not to catch up with anyone."

Bernie must have looked confused. It was a lot to take in, and he had already decided that Col. Anderson was the brooding, silent type. Too tough for words! Yet here he was talking.

"Just drive a little over the speed limit till we get to Blande Boulevard, then drive so you don't see anyone in front of you. Okay?" The man put his baseball cap on and pulled it low, over the bangs of the wig.

"Okay."

"When we get—aw, I'll explain the rest in the car. Here. What were you trying to shoot last night? The television?"

Bernie could only nod silently. He was too in awe of the rifle he was holding. It looked complicated. It wasn't like the toy Davy Crockett rifle he'd had as a kid. "I probably shouldn't shoot the TV, though."

"I don't have to tell you that you'll be able to afford a much better one when this is all done."

Bernie cradled the rifle, if not like a lover then perhaps like a baby calf. He started to set it in position, when the Colonel reached in quickly and flipped a switch on the rifle's side.

"Okay, now," Col. Anderson said.

And Bernie lifted the rifle to his shoulder.

6 Chief Wanamaker was having a great time. He ranted and fumed and strutted up and down his office. Oberman was an alarmist. He was bad for morale. He was fomenting panic in the streets.

"Chief, I just—"

Don't interrupt, Oberman!

Oberman could see, through the window, Campbell standing there, waiting, shifting from foot to foot, wishing (Oberman knew) he had a cigarette. The Chief had not bothered to draw the blinds, which is how Oberman knew he was enjoying himself.

"Let me see your phone, Oberman," he barked.

Oberman handed it over.

"You get Twitter on this thing?"

Of course he did.

"Not any more. Nancy! Give this to Sergeant Gaye. Lock it in his desk. Oberman can have it when he goes off duty.

Sergeant Gaye was not a sergeant; that's just what they called him. He wasn't even a police officer any more, just a retiree augmenting his pension by acting as "desk sergeant" in a precinct that had never had an actual desk sergeant. He just manned the front desk.

Oberman watched Nancy and his phone pass through the rows of desks and disappear through the door to the foyer.

"And I've got another surprise for you," the Chief continued.

7 Amber Meir wanted to give her sympathies, but she didn't want to get caught making a personal call from work. Prishtine made it very clear he did not like that. There was a window of time before work, though, when it was not too early, really, to call. A decent hour. Amber called.

If Bernie's phone, buried beneath blankets in his brother's room, had never been successfully powered off by Bernie's incompetent thumb—is that better or worse? If its generic ringtone was audible throughout the house—would this have made any difference?

Bernie and Colin had already left. They were already in the car. The phone rang, if it rang, to an empty building, and Amber left a heartfelt voicemail that no one would ever check.

8 Things that could go wrong: ¶ The car could have been locked, and Bernie could waste time fumbling for the keys while inquisitive neighbors ("was that a gunshot?") poured from their houses. So Colin had had Bernie open the doors ahead of time.

The car could fail to start—Colin had almost asked Bernie to start the engine and leave it running, but he decided the chance of it getting stolen were as great as the chance of the starter failing.

And the rifle—letting Bernie use the rifle! Bernie could turn and stone cold shoot him. But Colin had seen on cop shows that they could tell from powder marks on the hands if someone had been firing a gun. He needed Bernie's hands on the rifle. So as Bernie aimed at his TV, Colin stood right at Bernie's side, too close for the rifle to pivot around and face him. That should put an end to any nonsense.

The poor boy was practically weeping tears of joy as the shots missed the television and thudded against the wall. There was a billowing cloud of plaster, but Colin barely noticed it because he was too busy ducking away from the shells that came flying out of the side of the rifle. Not something he'd expected.

But it was only five shells. He snatched the rifle from Bernie's limp, quivering grasp, flicked the safety on, and popped the magazine out, letting it fall to the floor. He stuck another one in, and then draped a trash bag, the one with the banana peel in it, over the rifle. He already had the other trash bag over his wrist. Somewhat encumbered, like a Christmas shopper, he ushered Bernie by pressure on his shoulder out the door and over to the car. He intentionally left his duffel bag, tossed behind the couch.

"My arms are tingly," Bernie said inanely.

Colin pulled the passenger side door shut and scrunched himself down. He managed to tuck himself in so that he was actually sitting on the floor, his legs twisted around sideways. "Hurry up and drive," he hissed. The position was extremely uncomfortable, and the burner phone in his pocket dug into his thigh. He had the rifle out from under the trash bag, lying on the passenger seat, level with his shoulders. With a great deal of bumping of elbows, he removed his wig, his hat, his disguise accouterments, and tossed them all into the trash bag they'd come from, next to the banana peel and circular. He knotted the bag and slipped the Alfred E. Neuman mask on. The car started moving, and he heard the *flup-lup* of cardboard whipping off. From his seat on the floor all he could see was the sky flashing by. "Faster. Drive faster. Okay, now slow down."

"Don't irritate me, man," said Bernie.

"Are we on Rano?" Colin allowed himself to hoist his body up for a quick peek to see if the stolen car was still there. Someone had swiped it overnight, he noted with pleasure. Everything was going according to plan. "Drive down St.

Gabriel," he said then. "You can take Burris Avenue. You know where Michaelson Road is?" Colin had studied his map, of course.

"Of course I know—"

"Turn down it and when you get to the creek pull over to the railing." Colin was already cranking down his window. He felt the knotted trash bag to make sure there was nothing in it he'd need—no bullets, most importantly. There were two trash bags to keep track of, and he didn't want to make an elementary mistake.

When he felt the car stop, Colin tossed the knotted trash bag out the window without looking. He heard a splash. "Now drive on." There was a pretty good chance that his DNA was all over the wig, but even if anyone thought to follow the car's path to this place, the bag would have floated far downstream. And of course there was little to connect the wig to the Incident in the first place. "Take a left."

As they drove, Colin uncomfortably slid the tape holders full of magazines from the other trash bag. He set them on the passenger seat behind him. He felt the unearthly calm that settled upon him. They coasted up to a stop light, and he bullied Bernie into putting on his ridiculous mask.

"I look stupid."

"We're twins," said Colin. "You'll see how it works. Now look. When we get to Blande, or even right before it, roll down your window. You'll have to scooch down. I'm going to be leaning across you and shooting out the window right over you, which is going to be uncomfortable but it's only for a few minutes. Keep down, or just at a level where you can drive without crashing. Remember, it has to look like only one of us in the car."

"For surprise."

"Right, for surprise."

"Is this a good idea?" Bernie asked.

"Don't worry you'll do fine."

"If you see a green Volvo, I call dibs. A lady driving, someone next to her."

"Okay."

"An ugly someone next to her. Like deformed."

"Okay."

"Dibs."

"Okay."

"Is this a good idea?" Bernie asked again without pausing.

Colin exhaled. He felt calm, but he felt nothing else; and yet he felt like he might soon be feeling something else. His eyes were watching the sky, but he could tell, from the few trees that hove into view, that they were almost there.

"Bernie. Bernie, roll down your window," he said.

9 Oberman was being punished, which meant Campbell was also being punished, which meant Campbell was mad. ¶ The two of them had been assigned the absolute worst job a police officer could get. They had to go notify some civilian's mother that her son had died of an OD last night.

"You are going to pay for this," said Campbell.

"I'm already paying for this," said Oberman.

"Not yet you're not." Campbell was not driving, which meant he was chain-smoking, something, let us recall, he was not supposed to do in the patrol car, something no one was ever going to tell him not to do. Certainly not John Oberman.

"Look, I'll do the talking. You can wait in the car if you want." But Oberman did not want to do the talking. Silently—so Campbell would not make fun of him further—he was praying for a miracle. Anything to take him away from facing the mother and telling her her son was dead while she wailed and said, "Did you kill him?" Anything to put off this horrible task for just a little while longer.

10 Always Colin and Carol, always Bernie and John. There were other people in town, of course. There was that anonymous hack who'd searched for "cottinend" on Twitter one day back in January, found @CottinendKing, and

called it in to the police. There's that poor mother, not yet told, not yet grieving. There will be the 911 operators, standing by; not answering yet, but they will be. And there are all these citizens in all these cars—who can count them all?—and they are driving obliviously down Blande Boulevard.

11 It was after nine when Sp!der's mother's wall phone finally rang. Sp!der had to bolt from the basement, running, or at least jogging, up the stairs. His mother was shuffling towards the phone, but Sp!der skidded around her and snatched it away from her outstretched hand.

Ronnie's voice said, "Mickey? I can't talk long; I'm at work; but I have the info."

Sp!der was about to scream "about damn time" but he stopped himself. He could scream at her after she gave him the information.

"It was actually very hard to get. It took a lot of digging," Ronnie said.

"That doesn't actually make any sense," Sp!der thought. He also thought, "Come on, come on." But he only said, "Uh huh."

"The guy is named Bernard Feldstein."

Bernard Feldstein. And now, now Sp!der opened his mouth to scream at her; but Ronnie had already hung up.

"What was that all about?" Sp!der's mother asked. But her son had already dashed back to the basement door. *Bernard Feldstein.*

He considered stopping to research the name, present Oberman with a more complete dossier; but maybe now was the time for speed. "Deeds not words" was Sp!der's motto. He dialed Oberman.

And the phone rang and rang.

12 There was a small part inside Bernie that had figured it would not happen. It was too good. It was too bad. ¶ There was a small part inside Bernie that had not decided. Whatever he had said earlier was just provisional; his true mind not made up. Everything, was it not, was just provisional. He started to cry as he drove. He started to cry in part from discomfort and despair. He was jackknifed over in his seat, his face practically pressed directly into the steering wheel. His eyes peeked just over the horn, seeing, through the mask's ragged rubber eyeholes, very little. His hands, at ten and two, were in fact above his head. So hunchbacked was he at this moment that in order to face straight forward, his neck had to be tilted. "Titled up" is what it felt like, although his face was not up. It was horrible.

Riding on his back like a monkey, his elbow actually on his head, in his rubber hair, was the Colonel. Bernie could feel the weight of the gun, that terrible mass upon his shoulders. The Colonel was holding it, but the weight was on his shoulders.

He could hardly breathe in this position. He could wheeze a little. It was all he could do to keep the car on the road. His knees kept knocking against the steering wheel, or the dashboard, or his own left elbow. His right elbow was holding in place a plastic clip thing full of magazines wedged uncomfortably into his lap. He was completely helpless.

Mostly, therefore, he was crying from relief. Because he would not have to decide.

13 Oberman's phone began to ring in Sergeant Gaye's desk. It was the loud, irritating ring, a WAV file of an old-fashioned telephone. Gaye had no idea how to shut off a phone like this. He'd never even brought his own flip phone to work, and could hardly figure out why anyone would. He opened his top drawer and glanced at the screen, which was lit up, reading "Spider"—that was how Oberman had spelled it—and a 720 number. Then he slid the drawer closed and pointedly ignored the ringing until it stopped.

Three minutes later it began to ring again.

14 There are things you can only learn by trial and error, and practice. Colin knew that he was going to be passing cars quickly as they sped the other direction. If he squeezed the trigger when the target was "in his sights," so to

speak, it would be gone before he even fired. He had to lead the target, start shooting before it arrived in place. The first car he saw coming, as he got into position, was a minivan.

"You don't see too many of those any more," he said as he squeezed the trigger. Nothing happened. With a grunt of frustration at his own stupidity, Colin flipped the safety off and squeezed again.

It had been almost six months since his last practice shot. The shock he remembered, but the noise echoing in the car was louder. He could feel Bernie answering him—poor guy couldn't open his mouth without jostling Colin's arm, rested as it was on his head—but couldn't hear a word. He could not hear but could see the cartridges flying out sideways to clatter against the inside of the windshield and ricochet around the cabin. The rifle jerked upwards and Colin had to pull it down constantly. When the magazine ran out in a couple of seconds, the downward pressure he was exerting jerked the barrel down and he almost dropped the whole thing out the window. Perhaps he should have invested in a strap. Too late now.

Oh, and worst of all, he had fired most of his magazine off before the minivan even arrived. The jerking, battering of the bumpstock and the wobbling of Bernie's head had caused him to shoot erratically, and when the minivan passed he actually shot directly over its roof, over their heads. He could see the shocked faces of the passenger and the driver staring right at him. One of them was already pulling out his phone. By the time Colin wrestled the barrel back down he only had time for few bullets fired into the cargo space in back on the minivan. The rest of the contents from the magazine flew wasted across the median, across the street in its wake and into the woods. So much for no witnesses; the police would already be on the lookout, and no one was even dead yet. Worst of all, there were no other cars to be seen.

For a moment, Colin feared that the time change may have been fatal to his plan. Maybe no one went south on Blande Boulevard after ten A.M. While he thought this, though, his muscle memory was already ejecting one magazine—he threw it over his shoulder into the backseat—and snapping a replacement free from the tape holder on Bernie's lap.

"What the hell are you doing?" he heard Bernie shriek, but he was already back in position, rifle at his shoulder. No cars came.

16 First the radio squawked and a dispatcher gave a report that sounded too silly to be true, but then Oberman had the siren screaming. They were right nearby, heading north on I-81.

"It's *off*, somehow, that they call it a siren," Campbell said just to prove that he was unconcerned; in case lighting a cigarette as they serpentined around a corner was not unconcerned enough; "when *technically* the sirens had beautiful voices…"

Oberman didn't care what Discovery Channel special Campbell had watched last night. He didn't care where Campbell had picked up these annoying facts. "Just say we're on our way," Oberman said. He said it between gritted teeth, of course. Both his hands were spinning the wheel like a ferryboat captain.

"We're on our way over," said Campbell into the mic, and he couldn't help grinning. Honestly, weren't they both grinning?

16 When the rifle fired Bernie could feel the kick all down his spine. The jackhammering. It hurt his teeth. And that was before the earsplitting noise. He'd been to enough loud shows and loud bars he thought his hearing was already shot; but there was something particularly horrible about the explosions coming right above his ear, so fast they were less a percussion than a drone. And then the blazing hot brass casings came raining down upon him. "I am in hell," Bernie wept.

The halo of choking smoke had only begun to pool around the roof of the car.

17 Chugging down the avenue, a little Mazda Miata going thirty-five, forty m.p.h. max. An impatient queue tailgated behind it, no one *quite* leaning on their horn, but the feeling was there. On a long one-lane road with a median,

one bad actor can block the whole street and slow everyone down. Colin shook his head in sympathetic frustration. No wonder the street had been empty!

His first few shots fell in front of the Miata, and the rifle pulled up, but he was learning. He held his shot steady and let the vector of the cars move it into the path of the bullets: directly along the Miata, shaking the dimly glimpsed man driving it, and across the length of the vehicle, running right into the first tail-gater. The window shattered. A man's arms came up and then fell and after that he was out of sight, down the road.

What actually happens when you shoot a car: not once but a dozen times, say? Colin had had no idea, and it was something he intentionally did not research, in case a record of such research had proved suspicious. Could the car blow up? One lucky bullet in the gas tank, was that possible?

No car blew up; if the bullets hit a door, as opposed to a window, the damage just looked like little holes, like something minor. But Colin was dimly aware of the cars swerving as he passed, their drivers losing control. He ran out of bullets on the third car, and as he swapped a new magazine in he indulged in a glance over his left shoulder. The three cars he had hit were spinning off the road, running into trees, the embankment. Two cars slipped past as he reloaded, but one of them got billiard-balled by a caroming bullet-riddled metal coffin. The more cars he hit, the more everything seemed to escalate. Maybe something bad would happen to the ones he missed, too.

But Colin had already opened fire again. He caught two more cars, strafing the entire length of them, weaving up and down slightly right along the axis where the window met the door. There was a break in traffic, so he took his finger off the trigger. Just for a moment as his ears stopped ringing, he thought he heard shouts or screams. Now another car was coming—it looked like it had a whole family of five inside—so he emptied the remainder of the magazine directly into its screaming bowels.

There was a small straightaway, and it was clear that people could see, now, what was coming; but there was nothing they could do. One man in a sports car slammed on the brakes, but that just got him rear-ended before Colin strafed both him and the sedan that had struck him. A fat pickup turned to the left and screeched to a stop in the breakdown lane, its nose practically in the trees, its tailgate towards Colin. This was a pretty good plan, and Colin respected it: Could his bullets pieces the tailgate, whatever was on the flatbed, the cabin's rear wall, the seat, and then the driver, who was presumably ducking? Colin sent a burst his way, but he assumed the driver would live, and he couldn't begrudge him that.

Immediately behind the pickup, though, was a couple who just screamed and did nothing clever. Colin drew a line along their car, door-handle-height, and only for a flash could he see the two of them, their bodies jerking before they sailed on. Cars that pass, they pass really fast. It was hard to focus on what was happening across the way.

A brief pause and then around a curve came a man in a Volkswagen who just squinted in confusion at the carnage ahead. His window shattered and he died before he even processed it fully.

And so on. It wasn't bad, but Colin had expected a little bit more, honestly.

18

Bernie was pinned in one place. Even as the molten brass hailed, he could not move. He certainly could not move his head. A blazing hot shell rebounded and almost hit him in the eye; what if it fell into the eye-socket of the mask, wedged in there pressed against his bubbling pupil?

It didn't of course; it bounced off the rubber, like the rest of them. Only his hands were peppered with small burns, and he wondered why he wasn't wearing gloves. He wondered why the Colonel *was* wearing gloves; didn't this interfere with the fingerprint system? He couldn't ask, of course. It was too loud to ask anything.

The gunfire stopped for a moment, and then he had something else to say.

It was an oddity of his position that Bernie had to, *had to* keep his eyes on the road. He barely knew, if he knew at all, what was happening next to him or behind him. The southbound cars could have been exploding into flaming cartwheels for all he knew. It could scarcely be louder. But up ahead he could see. He could see the terrified eyes of each person approaching.

He could see the terrified eyes of whoever that lady that chauffeured Alan Jancewicz around was.

"Green Volvo!" he cried. "Green Volvo!"

19 This was the method he had practiced: He ejected a magazine, worked a new magazine free, snapped it home. ¶ The car was a little different from the basement, of course. He'd known it would be. In the basement he'd been careful with the spent magazines, but here in the car he could just toss them over his shoulder, out the window even. In the basement, the tape holder had sat on the cement floor, but here in the car he had to keep them on Bernie's lap. This wasn't so bad, usually, but when he ran through a tape holder worth of magazines, he had to bat it off Bernie's lap, reach back onto the passenger seat to get a new tape holder, wedge it into Bernie's lap—while Bernie complained about it, of course. Bernie complained about the smoke; Bernie complained about the hot shells. What did he think this was, a picnic? Colin was doing all the real work, anyway.

It was just that the cars whipped by so fast, and the magazines emptied so fast. As soon as one or two good cars peeled off, snaking their way to a crash, the bullets would just run out. So many cars zipped by unscathed. It all seemed like such a waste.

And now, after all that, the Volvo appeared? For a moment, Colin considered sparing whatever schmuck had called down Bernard Feldstein's wrath. He was cutting down an SUV right before the Volvo, and it would be simple to pretend he ran out of ammo, to let the green Volvo pass by.

But then he thought: Why not throw the poor guy a bone? Surely he owed Bernie this much? Colin kept the trigger down until the Volvo's windows exploded.

Really (Colin thought) what he wished he'd done was get a counter, like the kind the fire marshal used to tick off entrants into fairgrounds. What was the point without it?

He could tell they were nearing the end of their little run. The other thing he wished was that the trees were leafier. It really was a shitty April.

20 In front of Alan Jancewicz a Dodge Caravan suddenly started to swerve. There were rapid exploding noises. That Mercury Zephyr was approaching from the other direction.

"There are two people in that Zephyr," he explained to his mother. "You can only see one, but look how low it's riding. It can't be a heavy weight in the trunk because the front left wheel is the lowest."

His mother did not answer because she was screaming. The loud noises started again. The Zephyr sped closer and for a moment Alan was looking directly at a rubber freckled face before the window shattered.

The whole car went red as he closed his eyes.

21 As more information came over the transom, it started to sound less ridiculous and more horrific. Campbell stopped dropping the knowledge bombs he'd taken off his wife's Snapple caps. He still chain-smoked, faster and faster.

The dirt: A man in a rubber mask, possibly resembling Alfred E. Neuman, driving an old red coupe, has been shooting an automatic weapon at random across the median at southbound cars on Blande Boulevard. There was nowhere to turn off, no place to hide, no way, even, to warn motorists.

Oberman wove along I-81. Exit to Blande. "Left lane for southbound," Campbell said.

"If the perp is shooting across at southbound traffic, he'll be northbound."

"How are you going to catch him—"

But Oberman veered right.

22 Sometimes when the sun is bright and you close your eyes the light through the eyelids makes everything red. Maybe that was what was happening?

But then Alan opened his eyes, and no, there was blood in them. There was blood everywhere. His mother was slumped over, leaning forward like an off-duty marionette. Her shoulder belt held her up.

But what did Miss Gerri say? *Keep your eyes on the stage, Alan.* He looked away from his mother to see what was unfolding through the windshield. The car was still moving, that was one thing. It was in fact moving quickly and perhaps accelerating. Directly ahead a blue 2016 Toyota Camry was sliding into the median guardrail, bouncing off and spinning. The driver lolled and bled. Marionette.

Never had Alan been and never would Alan be allowed to drive a car. He knew the *theory* though; he knew all about how to drive a car. He'd watched a lot of YouTube videos. The first things he did was in fact intuitive. He reached out with his left hand and grabbed the steering wheel. Whipping it to the right he arced around the Camry. His car wobbled precariously. He was going too fast. Ahead waited a slalom of crashed, perhaps overturned vehicles.

Alan could see, very clearly, the pickle he was in. Blood kept trickling into his eyes, but he could see: that there was no way to stop. If he stopped, another driverless vehicle would just come zipping down the road and crash into him from behind. How many people had thought they were the lucky ones and gently slowed to a stop to avoid the pileup only to get hit from behind? Piled in.

The second pickle was that Alan's mother's foot was apparently on the gas pedal, and he couldn't reach it to knock it off without unbuckling his seat belt, something he knew he was never supposed to do while the car was moving. Between him and his mother was an emergency brake. He reached across his body and with his right hand pulled up the emergency brake.

It smelled bad, the skid, as the Volvo lurched sideways. Alan jerked the steering wheel. He squeaked to the left of a 2008 Chevrolet Silverado, coming up against the railing. The car started to rebound off it, but Alan dropped the brake back down, or "off," and drew the wheel towards him, keeping tight on the railing. Sparks flew up on his right. So many cars had bounced off the railing that there was a clear corridor for a ways here, if you kept close enough. He rode the railing past a large knot of wrecks, and swung hard to the left, jerking up the emergency brake again. If he could get the Volvo to swing around into the lee of this knot, it would be hard for anything except a tractor trailer to plow through everything and reach him here.

As the Volvo swung around, Alan saw a woman bleeding from her side, staggering around behind a 2009 Hyundai Sonata. He shifted into park and skidded partially around her before sliding to a stop. She could only stare at him, and he knew, as he locked eyes with her, that he should say something comforting to her. But the only thing he could think to say was, "In your face." She probably couldn't hear him anyway. It was a miracle he could hear anything with all the blood in his ears.

"In your—" he started and passed out.

23 Oberman came down the highway offramp, sirens blazing, and pulled directly across Blande, blocking it off. There was a long straightaway leading up to him.

Campbell was on the mic, trying to figure out where the other police were coming in. Oberman hopped out of the car, whipped out his badge and held it up as the first distant vehicle billied in closer. His hand was on his gun. He waved, with the badge hand, to the side of the road.

The car slowed to a stop in front of him, and the window eased down. "Pull over! Turn off your engine and wait! This is an emergency!" Oberman barked. He used the voice he usually reserved for second warnings. Just then Oberman could make out distant gunfire from the south. He took his hand off the gun and quickly waved the car on, around the patrol car. Another car was approaching, and in Oberman's estimation it was too close to him to be the source of gunfire. He gestured it through but then, when another one came, he waved this car over to the shoulder to be safe. "Stay there, I'll be with you in a moment."

He wondered for a moment if he should be heading towards the gunfire (which had now stopped)—but what was he going to do, ram the car? Shoot the tires out with his pistol? The perp should be pulling up any moment now. He sent one car after another to the side of the road. One of them had to be the one. And between the patrol car across the road and the civilian vehicles lining up along its side, no one was going to be breaking through this roadblock. Then all Oberman would have to do was check each car. Across the street ambulances went roaring south.

24 Colin eased up. As he shifted his weight, Bernie's head began to peek slightly up over the dashboard. "Keep down," Colin shouted, "but look up ahead. There'll be a red rag on a stake marking a break in the trees. Turn there. Run over the stake." His last words were drowned out by gunfire as he sprayed another couple oncoming cars. Was it too much to hope for that no one would see them turn off the road? "Slow down! The stake!"

"Is it my turn?"

"We'll switch seats here," Colin said, as he ducked in the window. Settling down on the overcrowded passenger seat, he pointed them out, the stake and the rag and the overgrown trail. The car jounced along the grass and the dirt and the shrubs, around the bend, behind the trees. Colin was pulling the magazine free, snapping another one in place.

The man in the Alfred E. Neuman mask unhunched its shoulders at last. He slowly sat straight up, cricking, first, his neck, back and forth. The mask turned towards Colin, who now had the rifle casually held across his lap, the bumpstock against his biceps.

Colin briefly squeezed the trigger.

The gun bucked. A bullet hit right below the mask, where the rubber flapped open against his collar. A flower of blood opened up. As the gun pulled up, the bullets drew a line right up the Alfred E. Neuman. The rubber billowed back and forth. It held most of the blood in, though a sequence of fine sprays misted back through the bullet holes. Colin leaned over and turned the keys. The car died.

That was more like it, to be honest. He wished they'd all felt like that.

But they hadn't, and now there was a lot to do quickly. Colin set the rifle, facing backwards, in Bernie's limp hand, his thumb in the trigger guard. He opened the passenger-side door. The ground looked firm enough, just last year's dead leaves. A garbage bag in his hand, Colin stepped gingerly out. He set the bag down and unzipped his coveralls with two hands simultaneously. The coveralls fell to the floor and he snapped them up. He dropped them into the bag, extracting, at the same time, the hooded windbreaker, which he draped over his arm.

The next step he had marked as optional, but he hadn't heard any sirens yet, and so he went for it. Leaning back into the car he grabbed—one, two, three, four —tape holders. One was partially shattered; one was still full of unfired magazines—such a waste!—and Colin shook those free. The tape holders went in the garbage bag. Slam the door. And he was off.

As he raced through the woods he slipped the windbreaker on and zipped it up on the run. Only when he pulled the hood up did he realize he was still wearing a mask. He pulled it off and stuffed it, as he ran, into the windbreaker pocket. Deep into the pocket—if it fell out that would be fatal.

Down the embankment in a flurry of dead leaves thrown up around him and whipping around in his wake. Only as he skidded up against the parking lot did he remember another reason he'd wanted the Incident to come off earlier: there'd have been fewer employees at Choice Pizza, fewer eyes to catch him coming out of the woods. He silently cursed Bernie and his arbitrary time changes.

But no one, as far as he could tell, saw Colin as he ran behind the dumpster. One flick of the thumb to unchain the bicycle and then he sped through the rear lot, out through the front lot, out into morning traffic along Route 434. One hand held the trash bag tight; it snapped back and forth in the wind. The hood of his windbreaker kept threatening to blow off, but he leaned forward, head down, and it never did.

Half a mile along he turned into the supermarket lot; there was a trash can outside the recycling room, he remembered, for people to drop in any cans and bottle that could not be recycled. The garbage bag went in, followed by his gloves. This was not even suspicious, really. And anyway, the supermarket was so far from Blande, by car at least, that the police shouldn't think of checking this trash can until long after it was emptied. He biked away, with traffic. At a light he checked his shoes and his hands to make sure there were no drops of blood, but he was clean. His face and neck the bike's mirror revealed to be clean as well.

Just a few more miles to his car, all of it downhill. If somebody had stolen it, or stolen the tires—it would be hard to explain, wouldn't it? But he skidded to a halt in front of an intact vehicle. He took his time easing open the levers and removing the front wheel. He was just a guy who drove down here and went for a ride. Much-needed exercise. The bike went in the back seat and Colin went into the front seat. He had no weapon on him. He had nothing to tie him to Bernard Feldstein, or Blande Boulevard, or the Incident. All he had to do was not act suspicious. He pulled his wallet out of the glove box, slipped it into his front pants pocket. Seat belt snapped in place, he eased into traffic.

25 The Blande southbound lane was completely backed up. There was a long queue of cars, too late for the massacre but quite trapped, and a patrolman had to back them up, one by one. Northbound must have been closed off, too, as no one was coming towards Oberman now; and then a patrol car approached. Oberman nodded in satisfaction.

"It's got to be one of these guys," Oberman told Lepage when Lepage rolled down his window. "There's no other way out."

"Don't be an idiot," said Lepage. "We found a coupe in the woods. Suicide."

Oberman borrowed Campbell's phone to take pictures of the plates, everyone along the side.

"Don't know how to use the camera; just never learned," Campbell monologued while Oberman finished up.

162

Then they let the cars go, and the two of them piled back in their black and white, and followed Lepage, wrong way down Blande northbound, to a pair of tire tracks leaving the road.

Down a curving trail, behind some trees, there was the perp dead in his car.

"Alfred E. Neuman, confirmed," said Lepage.

"Should we check to see if he's alive, like under the mask?" Oberman asked.

"Fuck him," said Campbell.

"He's not alive," Davis said. She had the passenger door open and was trying to look around without touching anything. "Look, he got the AR under his chin, pulled the trigger with his thumb. It shot him and kept firing auto-style. He's got at least a half dozen bullets in his face and head. He's a goner."

"That's weird," said Oberman. "It's got a bumpstock. How'd he shoot it on auto with the bumpstock facing away from him"

Davis shrugged. "Braced it against the seat. Probably thought he was just putting one bullet in him. Must've been a surprise!"

"Surprise my Aunt Fanny," Campbell snorted, which is what he'd say to anything.

"Jee-zus, look at all the shells. How many shots did he fire?" Oberman said.

"I'd say that confirms that this is the shooter's car," Lepage said.

Campbell said, "You had to ask? Just smell it in there."

"They say it's like an abattoir back on the road," Davis said. "Poor dumb bastards."

Oberman started to look around. The tire tracks trailed behind the car, through the churned-up leaves toward the road. Not all the way to the road, of course, because two patrol cars had pulled up behind it. It was hard to tell one set of tire tracks from the other.

"Not sure I'd call this shitpile a coupe," Campbell said.

As Oberman started to circle the vehicle, a third car pulled up. It was Chief Wanamaker. "Oberman, are you fucking up the crime scene?" he bellowed unnecessarily.

"No, chief."

"You and Campbell get out of here. You're on traffic detail. Go relieve Hope and Sanchez at the foot of Blande," he gestured with his cigarette. "Anyone trying to come north on Blande, send 'em down Maple to turn around. They'll tell you. Hey!" Now he was talking to Davis. "Leave it for the detectives."

Oberman with an exceptionally sullen Campbell maneuvered the car gingerly, on the narrow path, around the chief's. As they were pulling onto Blande some paramedics were coming up.

"Heard there was a deader," one said. He had to say it twice. At first Oberman assumed the man had a strange foreign accent, but then he noticed the horrible malignant growth on his jaw.

"Good Lord!" Oberman said.

"Yeah, I know. 'Kids, don't do drugs.' Don't be an asshole. Are we going up there of what?"

"Go take care of the civilians," Campbell said, leaning across Oberman. "Go on, kid," he added to Oberman. "Get us in position." They drove down Blande, southbound on the northbound side.

26 The traffic static from Ridgemont Road wafted across the parking lot. Closer was the peculiar rattling sound a shopping cart, one wheel frozen and rattling, made on the asphalt. A low murmur of customers counting their change or coughs from supermarket employees standing around holding cigarettes with their plastic deli gloves.

At the bottom of the trash can, in the pocket of a canvas jumpsuit, half-buried now beneath discarded circulars and vegetable bags, its battery critically low, Colin Lang's burner phone passively took in all these sounds.

The colloquialism *butt-dial* refers to an event, to which certain cell phones are prone: Pressure from one's body or the folds of one's pocket unwittingly depresses a button or two and dials a number, generally the last one called.

Carol Wernick's voice mail had been slowly filling up with a lengthy message that started with muffled voices discussing where to drive, and then how to drive, and then a green Volvo, and then everything is lost in the percussion of gunfire. Then the squeaking of a bicycle through traffic, and now the musique concrète of a supermarket parking lot, abruptly cut off with the battery's death.

27 Colin turned off 434, taking the long, looping route back to Blande. He wondered if he should pull over and change into his "good clothes," his spare work clothes from the trunk, now; he wanted to get these boots off him and into a garbage can; but he decided he'd better wait till he was on the highway. It would be less suspicious to change at a rest stop than some Cottinend side street.

As he got closer to Blande, Colin was disappointed to see that there was very little of the anticipated traffic snarl. All the reporters and rubberneckers were pulled over to the sides. Ambulances were coming by, from the other direction. There were the walking wounded, or the sell-shocked, looking for a reporter to talk to, looking for their few moments of fame. Colin wondered if he recognized any faces, but he couldn't be sure.

But that was all parked cars and foot traffic. No traffic jam, though. Instead, Colin could see ahead one cop car parked athwart the road, a cop telling everyone, as they approached with windows down, to turn off. The cop used big, sweeping cop hand gestures.

Colin wondered if he should just turn around now, himself. He could say Blande was closed, and it was the finding an alternate route that made him late. But he worried that pulling off now would look suspicious. Never turn around once the cops see you; that's what they say, right?

"What's the deal, officer?" he practiced saying. He pulled ahead slowly and rolled down his window.

28 The same name—"Spider"—had been calling all day, that 718 number, again and again. Gaye looked at the phone each time, closed the drawer each time, and each time waited it out, waited for the ringing to stop. It had to be something important; under ordinary circumstances he'd just call it over the horn —"Oberman, someone wants you"—but he knew Wanamaker would have his ass. Nevertheless, a combination of concern and annoyance—how *did* you turn off that rebarbative ringing?—inspired him to action. He looked up Campbell's cell number in the spiral directory. He slid close to him the big desk phone with the side row of clear buttons…

29 Traffic duty, while the King of Cottinend, so-called, was dead in his car a few miles away, was very frustrating for Oberman. There were not enough ambulances nearby, and he could hear backups being called from Binghamton and Ithaca. On the other side of the road, the south side, pooled a large margin of survivors, some mildly wounded and others just waiting to leave an official statement. Lepage was over there, trying to keep the press from coming too close and harassing everybody.

It was just another car to turn away. A white man, fortyish, in a hooded jacket, his window rolling down as Oberman leaned in to say, once again, that there was a police action ahead; take a right; detour; etc.

"What's the deal, officer?" the man said, but Oberman barely noticed. It was the smell instead, the smell that clung to the man's rumpled hair.

"Please step out of the car," Oberman said. His tone of voice had Campbell dropping his cigarette, looking up.

"Wait, is there a problem, officer? I'm just trying to—"

"No problem, sir, I'm just going to have to ask you to step out of the car." He put his hand on his pistol, unsnapping the holster. It was the smell of gunfire. Oberman knew it well, from the practice range, and most recently as a the concentrated stench in that red coupe…

"I don't know what the problem is, officer." He slowly extracted himself from the car. He stank.

"What's that in your pocket, sir?" Oberman said.

"My wallet? Oh, this? Oh." There was a bulge in the man's jacket. Oberman just reached in and pulled out a rumpled rubber mask. Alfred E. Neuman.

Everyone seemed to freeze.

30 Alan was dimly aware of voice coming down from the top of a great pit. He was at the bottom of the pit. The voice said, "We have a live one." ¶ It was very bright—the light, it turned out that two men were shining in his eyes.

"Scalp laceration. Looks like a ricochet?"

Alan should probably tell them something.

"Lord love a…look, there's metal in here. Dude's got metal plates in his head."

Well of course he does, though Alan. He is I. But that's not what he wanted to say.

"Saved his frigging life."

The lips of this corpse he controlled were moving, but it seemed there was no breath. He tried to gather his breath.

"Don't worry, guy, you'll be all right. You're in good hands."

"Two," said Alan.

"Don't try to talk."

"Two men. In the Zephyr."

31 Colin felt like—he felt like he had done this all before. He started to feel like he must have done everything right, if it had brought him to this moment. He was just watching for them to forget something, to leave something unattended; like their car keys, for example. Pennsylvania was closer than it ever had been.

167

The younger cop turned to gape at the mask, which dangled from his hand like a severed head. Like a picture Colin had seen in an art museum once—that Doré exhibit? The older cop, ten feet away or so, took a step forward. Everyone had a ridiculous, pop-eyed face except (he assumed) himself.

As the younger cop turned, Colin saw his open holster.

No one was prepared for this except Colin Lang. Colin Lang was prepared for anything. That gave him a moment's lead time.

He whisked the pistol from the holster, making sure to draw it up and out. He'd never drawn a pistol before, but he figured from his angle it would be easy for the tip to catch on the holster's edge. He pulled it straight up, and then stepped back. Don't waste time, he thought, on the unarmed cop. Colin was looking directly at the pistol, and not at anyone else; if the safety was not obvious, he'd be in trouble.

It was obvious.

He turned the gun towards the older man, who had taken the moment to begin drawing his own sidepiece. He'd had to unsnap his holster, though, and Colin had the drop on him. He started firing. The first shot went wild, but the cop was so close now there was really no way the second and third bullets could. The older cop wheeled, his gun firing wild as he spun to the ground. The young cop had stepped forward to grab Colin, and one of those wild shots hit him. He fell down at Colin's feet.

Lucky break, Colin thought. But as long as the old cop was still able to shoot, even at random, he was a threat. Colin wasted a couple of bullets on him. Ludicrously, as the shots went home, the cop's cell phone began to ring. "La Cucaracha." It was like shooting a target at the county fair to make a bell ring.

Satisfied, Colin turned back to the car and immediately fell down. The young cop, gripping his bleeding belly, had Colin's ankle in his other hand.

From the ground, Colin looked back at the younger cop's face. His eyes were shut and he seemed to be in pain; but his grip was strong. Colin pointed the gun at the cop's face.

He wasn't sure if he'd shot off five bullets or six. He also wasn't sure if cop guns held six bullets or if that was just cowboys'. It was exciting, though. He was excited to find out.

It turned out cop guns held a lot more than six bullets.

He pulled his leg from the slack dead grip, clambered to his feet. But then something knocked the wind out of him. He fell to the ground. He'd been so intent on the two cops, he hadn't really been focusing on the background screams. There'd been so many background screams today. But now some of what he'd been hearing registered.

"That's him! That's the guy."

Colin was offended! Didn't they know that Bernie was dead in a car a few miles from here? Why should they take this out on him?

And indeed most of them were running away or playing dead. But a couple of guys—thrill seekers, no doubt—had charged forward. One was wrapped around Colin's waist as they rolled in the grass. Another grabbed his feet, both feet, while a third wrapped himself around his shoulders and neck.

"You shot my brother, you asshole!"

"That was someone else," said Colin. "These dirty cops, for example." But it was hard to say things with these three people on top of him. And once everyone saw that the three people had him pinned, they all came over. Big heroes, jump on a subdued man.

"Where's the gun?" one of the geniuses said.

"I think he dropped it."

But Colin had not dropped it. It was in his hand, which was lodged under his chest, which was pressed into the dirt by the weight of a pig pile.

"I've got him covered," someone said. Someone had picked up the older cop's gun from the ground and was trying to act like a big man.

With a sigh of resignation, Colin waited until everyone had settled into their respective positions. In some tree some bird was blathering on, but everyone else was still. Only then did Colin pipe up: "Let me go! There are lives at stake."

169

"I've already called the police," a reassuring voice nearby said.

"There's no time for that. Listen! This is only one of the several mass shootings people dressed as cops—terrorists—they're pulling off today. Look, you saw what direction I drove up from. It was the opposite way. I just got here too late to stop this one, and I'll be too late to stop the next if you don't let me up. That's all. You need to get me to the elementary school."

Colin tried to apply all the lessons he'd learned about lying. Don't give too much information. Remember everything you say. Keep a low, authoritative voice—that had seemed to work well. And perhaps it was working now.

"The elementary school?"

"Yes, Burton Elementary. You know where that is?"

"My—my daughter goes there."

"I obviously," Colin continued, "didn't do this. I shot no one innocent. The fact that I came driving up from the south should be proof enough. I'm the only thing standing between this town and three hundred dead children, and right now you're killing them! If you don't trust me, just put me in you car, one of you. You can drive. Drive like the devil is after you, and we can still make it on time."

"I'm calling Burton," the reassuring voice said, but no one seemed to think that action was enough. Everyone—they acted as one, didn't they? looking at each other constantly for confirmation—started to ease a little, just a little.

"I," suggested one man who was sitting on Colin's neck, "have a fast car. I know how to get there."

Another: "We can grab some handcuffs off the cop. Make sure this guy doesn't try anything funny."

Yet another: "The cops *were* acting a little *off*, weren't they?"

And just as the pile of bodies started to shift and Colin could breathe somewhat easily again, a screaming sound, the sound of sirens, tore through the still morning.

"Let me up," said Colin, "so I can make sure they're on out side."

But the spell was broken. "Give it a moment," someone, everyone said.

Two and then three cop cars skidded up. By craning his neck, Colin could see that the police, as they leaped out, sheltered their fat bodies behind their car doors. They looked ridiculous, crouched like action heroes in their ill-fitting sweaty uniforms.

"Officer down!" one cried, lamely. But the rest of them were shouting other things. One by one, their hands in the air, people peeled away from Colin's prone form. "I'm unarmed! I'm unarmed!" each one said. One of them, the big man, actually set the second pistol gingerly on the ground and stepped away from it.

Colin thought hard, but there was only one thing he could come up with. The police were too well shielded. But everyone else was just standing there, their hands up like idiots. As soon as the last man obediently clambered off, Colin rolled over. The gun was already in his hand; a second one lay nearby. It was harder to aim than the rifle, especially while flat on his back, but everyone was much closer.

He was almost out of bullets when they finally came out from behind their doors and shot him dead where he lay.

32 Carol woke before noon into a surreal landscape she didn't recognize as her own room or even, for a moment, Colin's. ¶ Then she remembered: Colin's wild if theoretical night out and her own shameful hours of pining for him like a schoolgirl. Here she'd slept in her clothes, too. She felt stale and gross, but the thought of taking a shower and putting the same clothes back on felt even grosser. The mystery of Colin Lang remained unsolved, and perhaps she'd never solve it.

She was preparing to leave when she discovered that she had neglected to plug in her phone last night. The battery was dead. An old caution forbade her from leaving the house with no phone, so she went to the kitchen and, as she had so many time before, plugged into Colin's charger. Then she remembered Colin's phone, and the voice mail. There was only a moment of conscience-wrestling before she played the message. It was from Colin's mother, calling to say that he should come a little late the next day, as she was scheduled for some kind of test in the morning. Carol deleted the message and set the phone next to her own on the kitchen counter, planning on plugging it in once she charged up.

While she waited she made a pot of coffee. Idly she wandered into the living room with a steaming mug—it literally had a Radcliffe Worth Partners logo on— and put on the TV. Some kind of breaking local news was interrupting the networks. A mass shooting right here in Cottinend. She could hear sirens in the distance, getting louder; could it be nearby?

Carol Wernick blew across the top of her coffee as she sat down. The sirens were louder now, too loud, really, but Carol's focus was on the newscaster. With the attention of someone who has lived so long by numbers, she settled back to wait for the count of how many had died.

ABOUT THE AUTHOR

I don't think Hal Johnson is a very unusual sort of a guy. He's just—well, the average American citizen and family man, the kind that are the backbone of the nation. I admire him and like him. I like his attitude. Until, that is, he gets behind the wheel of an automobile. At that point he changes. He changes from a careful, considerate citizen—to a menace.

•"Driven to Kill," 1948 driver's safety film.

ALSO BY THE AUTHOR (THAT MENACE!)

Immortal Lycanthropes
Fearsome Creatures of the Lumberwoods
The Big Book of Monsters
Impossible Histories
Sudden Glory
Apprentice Academy: Sorcerers
Apprentice Academy: Knights
I Was a Soldier: Poems

haljohnsonbooks.substack.com

www.ingramcontent.com/pod-product-compliance
Lightning Source LLC
Chambersburg PA
CBHW071516170626
46811CB00007B/2874